THE MONSTER OF TWENTY MILE POND

"A fantastical novel with a mysterious creature and added thrill of a murder, Rowe creates a connection with the reader through sympathy, mystery and an overall amazing story." — TINT OF INK

"Rowe is an excellent writer and you can't really go wrong reading anything by him. This is one of his best." — THE PEI GUARDIAN

"Rowe's writing shines particularly brightly when his lawyer is chastising the (female) premier or other political discussions are underway, but the entire book is a rollicking ride with likable characters (except the skeets) in familiar settings."
— THE NORTHEAST AVALON TIMES

"A well-constructed novel, weaving murder and monsters into a single speculative tale." — THE PACKET

THE PREMIERS JOEY AND FRANK

"A voyeuristic and tantalizing trip through the workings of the government by a man who was there." — THE PILOT

"Rowe's stories paint not only an interesting picture of Rowe's own life, but the lives of the two men in which the book is named, and in the process, their greed, power and lust." — THE MUSE

"*The Premiers Joey and Frank* is crack for political junkies and will be a welcome gift for even the marginally interested observer of the political scene." — THE TELEGRAM

ROSIE O'DELL

"*Rosie O'Dell* is one of those books with such brilliant writing as to lull you into forgetting you're actually reading." — THE PILOT

"Yes, it's Bill Rowe—back this time with his third novel, which I think is by far his best. Probably one of the better novels to come out in the past few years—depending on your own tastes, of course."
— THE NORTHEAST AVALON TIMES

"[A] deeply emotional page-turner by one of the country's finest writers." — MEGAN MURPHY, INDIGO

"This is a terrific story that hinges on a woman who is like quicksilver, running through all the cracks." — THE GLOBE AND MAIL

"It's well-written (Rowe is an experienced and accomplished writer), the characters are excellently drawn and much of the writing is just plain funny." — THE PEI GUARDIAN

"There is not a false note in this book. All the characters are drawn with skillful insight, the descriptions are so vibrant you can almost hear the water and feel the mist of St. John's, Newfoundland. Although it has elements of a thriller, this is no gothic soap opera, but rather a brilliantly crafted look into the hearts and souls of ordinary people who are thrown into extraordinary circumstances."
— ATLANTIC BOOKS TODAY

"This novel is a real page-turner, with lots of tension and mystery."
— THE TELEGRAM

DANNY WILLIAMS, PLEASE COME BACK

"I started to really appreciate Rowe's ability to narrow down a topic and come up with something pithy and witty to say about it, week after week." — THE TELEGRAM

"Like any columnist worth his salt Rowe is provocative and a number of the columns deal with topics whose lessons are still relevant."
                    — THE NEWFOUNDLAND QUARTERLY

"Rowe's columns on Williams's persona, bellicose manner and political antics truly shine. What Danny Should Do in the Crab War? (May 7, 2005) puts a delightful Shakespearian twist on Williams's strategic positioning; Is Danny a Dictator? (June 25, 2005) will stand as a classic." — THE CHRONICLE HERALD

"A brisk read and a fine book to have in your personal library."
                    — THE COMPASS

"[Rowe] does it all, of course, with his usual blend of droll good humour and common sense." — THE GLOBE AND MAIL

"With a mind—and a pen—as sharp as a paper cut, the elegant, affable Rowe remains Newfoundland's literary agent provocateur, provoking, teasing, sometimes coddling his subjects, but all the time digging towards truths that cause discomfort for the province's Who's Who and everyman alike." — THE BUSINESS POST

DANNY WILLIAMS: THE WAR WITH OTTAWA

"Interesting book about a successful Canadian politician . . ."
— THE GLOBE AND MAIL

"[Danny Williams] is captivating. [Bill Rowe] spares no punches."
— THE COMPASS

"The most interesting political book to be released in Canada in
some time . . ." — THE BUSINESS POST

"Rowe's Ottawa chronicle [is] absorbing, humorous."
— THE TELEGRAM

"I quickly realized that this was not going to be a dry political memoir. To the contrary, not only is the book interesting and revealing of
this contentious time, it is very funny in places."
— THE CHRONICLE HERALD

"An exciting read." — THE NEWFOUNDLAND QUARTERLY

"[One of] three of this year's most controversial and talked about
political books." — THE HOUSE, CBC RADIO

"Rowe has a more humanistic side to politics. It is as if a citizen managed to be a fly on the wall while Danny Williams fought."
— CURRENT MAGAZINE

"An eye-opening, often hilariously funny, account of life among Ottawa power brokers and civil servants."
— CANADIAN LAWYER MAGAZINE

"Bill Rowe has a lot to say. There are dozens of interesting stories told, and comments passed on . . ." — THE NORTHEAST AVALON TIMES

"A fascinating and frequently funny read." — DOWNHOME

"Written with the knowledge and insight that only an insider could possess, this book (sub-titled 'The Inside Story of a Hired Gun') is a timely reminder of the duplicity of far too many of our elected leaders—no matter what their political stripe."
— ATLANTIC BOOKS TODAY

"The writer's good English style—rare today—his knowledge of all kinds of personalities in the political world and his misadventures in getting a basic office set up (which took six of the eight months he was there) all make for amusing and exciting reading."
— THE PEI GUARDIAN

THE TRUE CONFESSIONS OF
A BADLY
MISUNDERSTOOD
DOG

BY BILL ROWE

THE TRUE CONFESSIONS OF A BADLY MISUNDERSTOOD DOG

THE MONSTER OF TWENTY MILE POND

THE PREMIERS JOEY AND FRANK

ROSIE O'DELL

DANNY WILLIAMS, PLEASE COME BACK

DANNY WILLIAMS: THE WAR WITH OTTAWA

IS THAT YOU, BILL?

THE TEMPTATION OF VICTOR GALANTI

CLAPP'S ROCK

Bill Rowe

THE TRUE CONFESSIONS OF

A BADLY MISUNDERSTOOD DOG

FLANKER PRESS LIMITED

ST. JOHN'S

Library and Archives Canada Cataloguing in Publication

Rowe, William N. (William Neil), 1942-, author
    The true confessions of a badly misunderstood dog
/ Bill Rowe.

Issued in print and electronic formats.
ISBN 978-1-77117-441-1 (paperback).--ISBN 978-1-77117-442-8
(html).--ISBN 978-1-77117-444-2 (pdf).--ISBN 978-1-77117-443-5
(html)

    I. Title.

PS8585.O8955T78 2015   C813'.54   C2015-905949-6
                                                C2015-905950-X

PRINTED IN CANADA

RECYCLED
Paper made from
recycled material
FSC® C103567

This paper has been certified to meet the environmental and social standards of the Forest Stewardship Council® (FSC®) and comes from responsibly managed forests, and verified recycled sources.

Cover Design by Graham Blair

FLANKER PRESS LTD.
PO BOX 2522, STATION C
ST. JOHN'S, NL
CANADA

TELEPHONE: (709) 739-4477   FAX: (709) 739-4420   TOLL-FREE: 1-866-739-4420
WWW.FLANKERPRESS.COM

9 8 7 6 5 4 3 2 1

    Canada Council   Conseil des Arts
                       for the Arts   du Canada

We acknowledge the [financial] support of the Government of Canada. *Nous reconnaissons l'appui [financier] du gouvernement du Canada.* We acknowledge the support of the Canada Council for the Arts, which last year invested $153 million to bring the arts to Canadians throughout the country. *Nous remercions le Conseil des arts du Canada de son soutien. L'an dernier, le Conseil a investi 153 millions de dollars pour mettre de l'art dans la vie des Canadiennes et des Canadiens de tout le pays.* We acknowledge the financial support of the Government of Newfoundland and Labrador, Department of Tourism, Culture and Recreation for our publishing activities.

To my grandchildren,
Rowan, Elizabeth, and Phoebe,
who inspired this book.

THE TRUE CONFESSIONS OF

A BADLY

MISUNDERSTOOD

DOG

Chapter 1

When I was Human

My name is Durf and I am a dog. I can freely admit that now, but for a long time I thought I was human. I played with the other kids in my house as if I was one of them and, no matter what I did, they would laugh and clap their hands and hug me and beg me to do it again. The adults, though, were another story. I never knew when they might go weird on me. Gross overreaction seemed to be built into their natures. Don't get me wrong, I loved our grown-ups dearly. But they were a constant challenge. Here's one example, just for starters, of what I was up against, right in my own home, during those days when I was human.

At the time I was still a growing boy and weighed no more than sixty pounds, tops. It was late afternoon, and I was taking my nap on the soft sheets of a bed upstairs in our house. I was used to the beds because the kids often smuggled me into them when the grown-ups weren't looking, and so I sometimes took a nap in one during the day. I couldn't let such cozy spaces go to waste all day when no one else was using them.

I'd jump up on the bed and root the covers off with my nose. And no matter what the grown-ups claimed, there weren't that many drips left on the sheets or pillows from my nose, and not a whole lot of mud from my paws. And the heaps of my shedding fur weren't always as huge as they claimed, either. Certainly not enough for a deafening shout. "No, Durf, get off that bed—Good Lord, just look at all the dirt and fur—and stay off, I said!"

A person who didn't know my family might have thought that such a bellow from one of the grown-ups might have been a bit upsetting, but I didn't mind too much. I could tell from the kids' gigglings that we were just playing one of our games, probably. I'd slide off the bed and lie low downstairs for a while. Then I'd climb the stairs, silently, and jump back in.

Now, on this particular day it wasn't a shout that woke me up from my nap on the bed, but the sound of chattering voices downstairs. Suddenly my sniffers took in this delightful fragrance. Granny's cologne! I hadn't smelled it for days, and it made me stand up on the bed with joy.

The last time she'd visited, I crept up behind her while she bent over in the porch taking off her boots, and in a gesture of love and affection, I rooted her with my snout. She jumped up in the air, pretty high for a woman in her golden years, and grabbed the back of her skirt with both hands and yelled at me in short, punchy words that made her sound delightfully more feisty and saucy than I'd ever seen her. Her other grandchildren grinned and tittered at the fun we were having.

That memory filled me with such love now that I jumped off the bed. I heard her asking, "Where's that foolish Durf?" She couldn't wait to begin to play. I bounded down the stairs to greet her. The whole family was sitting in the living room gabbing when

I entered. Granny put a playful look of startled terror on her face when I bounced gleefully toward her, my tail—indeed my whole rear end—wagging vigorously. My tail struck something on the coffee table, and a plate of cookies went flying across the room, landing upside down on the carpet, followed by the teapot and cups. No big deal—I could easily gobble up all the cookies to the last crumb and lick the tea off the carpet afterwards.

I jumped right up on Granny's lap and sat there looking cute like the other little grandchildren always did. Of course, what I hadn't expected her to do was hold her glass of wine in my way as I jumped up, so that it flew out of her hand. The wine landed on the front of her dress and all over her face and eyeglasses and hair on the way to the wall. I started licking her face and eyeglasses clean of the wine. But instead of letting me finish the job, the sweet little lady jumped to her feet and, without meaning to, I'm sure, dumped me rather roughly off her lap onto the floor.

At first I was confused and hurt to hear the grown-ups shouting, "No, Durf, stop," and, "Bad Durf, bad, bad Durf," and being led somewhat abruptly by the collar out to the backyard. But it was plain how the other kids felt about my part in the event: they were struggling not to smile too much or break out in giggles. And they came outside to play with me and said nice stuff like, "That's all right, Durf. It was only a little misunderstanding."

So, I soon loved Granny and the other grown-ups in the house as much after as before. But the experience did set me to wondering about whether I was different from the other kids. I couldn't make up my mind that day, and it took another outstanding event later to make it clear to me exactly what I was.

Chapter 2

How I Got My Famous Name

Before I come to all that, though, I know you've been wondering how on earth I got a beautiful name like "Durf." Well, I was just a toddler when I chose it, by a stroke of good luck, on the very same day that I adopted my family.

There were four people in my family besides me: Nice Boy, Nice Girl, Nice Woman, and . . . That Man. Right from the start, That Man acted as if he was the head guy around the house. And for some reason, it bugged me. Yeah, I know, right—who died and made him boss? What I didn't understand at the time was that my reaction was just my genuine "top dog" nature starting to come out in me. And, as we shall see, his takeover attempts did not meet with great success.

Nice Woman and That Man were the mother and father of Nice Boy and Nice Girl. I was responsible for Nice Boy and took him under my care. Nice Girl had gerbils in a cage in her room at the time, which she and I liked to watch as they ran in their exercise wheel and explored nooks and crannies in their living space. I really liked the fact that the gerbils were not always out of their cage trying to take control of the whole house like the two other so-called "pets," those cats, who were soon to invade the place and throw my life into an uproar.

That first day in my house I was sitting on the floor, waiting for Nice Boy to throw the ball again. While I was looking eagerly at the ball in his hand, I wasn't yet able to sit up straight on my haunches, but slewed off to one side lopsidedly, resting on one haunch, with the other hind paw sticking out. I was glad to hear him and Nice Girl saying how cute and funny they found that. We kids were going to fit in well together here in our house.

Whenever I chased the ball I would slip and slide on the hardwood floor, often tipping right over on my back and waggling my legs in the air, struggling to get right side up again. I liked making them laugh and pat me and pick me up and hug me. They weren't just my new brother and sister; they had also become my best friends. And I learned at the start how smart Nice Boy was when he zeroed right in and said, "Just look at the size of his paws. I've never seen paws so big on a little puppy like this."

As I'd learned from my mother, I responded graciously to him by saying, "Wrurf." Which meant, "Well done, my fine lad. We'll go far together, under my guidance."

Then That Man butted in: "Yes, I don't want to frighten everyone to death, but I dread the day when the rest of his body actually grows into those paws. We'll have to double the size of the house."

Really sarcastic-like, right? Now, don't get me wrong. I loved That Man and would take a bullet for him any day, but the minute I arrived here I got a bit of a bad vibe from him. His inflated ideas about being in charge in these parts put a strain on our relationship—not deep down in the relationship because we always knew we'd gladly die for each other, but on the surface, when his insecurity around me made him show off and act like he was Mr. Big. But there could only be one leader, as I'd already learned at my mother's knee back at the kennel, and I'm not telling you dogs who are hearing my story anything new—you've all been through this—when I say that if there were going to be any bosses around this household, they were going to be me.

Looking back, I can't believe how advanced in my thinking I was, before I even knew I was a dog. Right from the beginning, to get my feelings across to That Man loud and clear, I said to him, "Rauwufff," meaning "Listen here, my bucko, you'll find out all about dread when I do grow into these paws."

He responded most inappropriately. He came over and took my paws in both hands and examined them closely with a goofy smile on his face, and he showed no sign of submission whatsoever. Next he rubbed my floppy ears, causing me to involuntarily lick his hand. He was none too sharp, I could see, when it came to proper behaviour. By the looks of things, I had a lot of work ahead of me to straighten out That Man and make him learn his place in this world. You'd never say from our shaky start that he'd end up helping me tell this fascinating story of my life of adventure, fun, sadness, and laughter. I only hope he's gets everything right.

That first day, Nice Girl said to Nice Boy, "What are you going to call him? A great puppy like him needs a really cool name." I could tell she was extremely smart, too. I couldn't believe how lucky I was to get them as my brother and sister.

Instantly, a lot of great names went through my head. First, Chicken Cacciatore came to mind. That was from my time at the kennel, before I adopted my family, when the lady who was looking after us there dropped her box of lunch on the floor, and I courteously rushed to get to it and licked it empty for her, to save her the trouble of having to pick it up. The way she shouted out, "Oh my heavens, he ate my chicken cacciatore!" made me think, yes, that sounded, and tasted, like a good name.

I had also heard the name Prime Rib Roast on her TV set and saw it sitting there glistening in its roaster. It certainly had a good look to it, even though I couldn't smell it. What a first-rate name it would have been came later, when Nice Woman left the kitchen for a minute and I jumped up on a chair to sample the roast beef on the counter for her. When she came back she saw me giving it a tremendous vote of confidence with my mouth, so I don't know why she dumped it into the garbage. I'm sure I got it across to her that her roast was absolutely delicious. In any case, I didn't get named Prime Rib Roast.

My mother had taught me other wonderful possibilities for names during our feedings at the kennel. She told me about the good old days of long ago, which she'd heard about from her own mother and grandmother, when our ancestors were rootless, roaming mongrels known as the St. John's water dog. That was before some Lord High Mucky-muck across the ocean got fancy on us and started calling us Labrador retrievers. When we were the old water dogs, she said, we developed our famous, justly admired webbed toes to help us swim out in the oceans and ponds and rivers and rescue people all the time. I kept hoping, after I adopted my family, that one of these days I'd get a chance to rescue That Man from drowning. It might make him stop being so pigheaded and stubborn and understand my supervisor role better. As fate ordained it, I did get an opportunity to rescue him from the water, later, but as you will see, owing to his usual lack of team spirit, it ended badly.

But back to possible good names. My mother told me that one of the favourite pastimes of the old water dogs was to sneak under the cutting tables where fishermen were gutting and beheading codfish. There we could have our fill of the cod's offal and innards they tossed to the ground: real gourmet grub she called "Fish Guts." Yes, that would have been a pretty good name.

Back in those days, too, she said, we developed the wonderful talent of being able to look innocent as we passed any dried cod, or caplin, or a bucket of salt beef, and then suddenly bolt sideways to grab a mouthful and take off for the woods or under a shed, whatever hideout was available, and dine away to our heart's content.

People seemed to appreciate our talents in those days, Mother said, judging by the way they cheered us on as we sped away, like, "Get going, you mangy mongrel," or, "Yes, you'd better run, you thieving cur." So, those names would have been a couple of attractive ones from the olden days, Mangy Mongrel or Thieving Cur.

I heard another good name the day my family and I were invited to a fancy luncheon party out at Granny and Grampy's country cottage. The name sounded best when it was said with real passion, as it was that day: "You Moronic Mutt!"

Their cottage was an excellent place for having a snooze in front of the door where the sun shone right on you, warm and cozy, and people going in and out, especially Granny, gave you a wholehearted poke of affection with their toe, grumbling in fun that they had to make a high, wide step over you.

Now, Granny and Grampy had this sausage-shaped dog named Zippo. He was about as tall as a medium-sized rabbit but more than twice as long. When I asked him how come he was named

Zippo, he looked at me like I was crazy and said, "What? Haven't you ever seen me run?" And he zipped around the field behind the house on his stubby legs, doing a flat-out gallop of about one mile an hour. While he was hurtling along, I walked circles around him, but I disguised that by jumping and prancing as if I were struggling to keep up with him.

Only a few times did I accidentally knock him off his feet, and since he didn't have far to fall on those short little legs, there was no real need for Granny to yell out, "Durf! You stop knocking Zippo down." I wondered why she never said a word to Zippo when he bit my ear every chance he got. And those bites didn't tickle, either, in case anyone was wondering why I let out the yelps, which Granny must have misunderstood, because she just smiled at Zippo and said, "Good dog."

Now, on this day in the country, while Granny and Grampy and all of the guests were out on the front lawn with their glasses of wine, Zippo invited me to go with him into the kitchen. "I want to show you a feast for your eyes," he said, "and if you play your cards right, a feast for your mouth, too. Give me a hand here." Up on his hind legs, he extended his full length against the closed kitchen door in a way that looked like he was familiar with the operation. I joined him in pushing, and together we made the door creak open. Instantly, a fragrant wave from paradise burst out.

"I was wondering where the great smell was coming from," I said, following him in.

"Yes, that would be the glazed ham up there on the counter," he said. "Granny just finished baking it for me. Now, normally I'd jump up to it without more ado and get it myself, but I wanted you to be part of the fun this time, since you're my guest. That's why I brought you in here." I looked at his stumpy little legs and the height of the counter and—call me suspicious, but I figured he just might have brought me in here for another reason. I didn't say anything, though, because the bouquet hitting my nostrils made me overjoyed that I was having this chance to buddy up with him on this job. "What you need to do is reach up there and grab the ham," he went on, "and we'll drag it outside to the field and devour it. Any questions?"

"Not one," I said. But then, for some unknown reason, a picture of Granny hopping up and down in a rage popped into my head. "Well, one question. Are you sure this will be all right with Granny?"

"Oh my goodness, yes," he said. "I've done this a hundred times. She'll love it. You know how cute she thinks everything I do is? Well, this is her favourite thing for me to do."

"Okay, but I can't reach the ham from the floor where it's so far back on the counter," I said. "I'll have to hop up on that chair and stretch in and get it."

"That's a good idea. That's what I always do."

"Is that how you got stretched? Ha ha ha."

"Knock it off with the lame jokes," growled Zippo, "and hurry up before Granny comes in."

"I thought you said she won't mind."

"She won't. But if she sees that I want it, she'll put it in my feeding dish. Then you won't get any. Is that really what you want to happen here, Durf? Me getting it all and you getting none?"

"Oh my jumpin's, no, that would be tragic."

"I thought not. And ham tastes better out in the field in the open air. Plus we can have a bit of fun playing a game with it, trying to tug it away from each other. But here's the big bonus. We can drive those crows out there crazy when they see the feast we've got and that they can't have any of it."

"Perfect, Zippo. You're great at planning stuff out. You should be prime minister. That Man was watching the news on television the other night and he said, 'Good Lord, it would be better if Durf was prime minister.' But I think you'd be even better still. Okay, here goes. Lean up against the chair and keep it steady while I reach in for it. Good. Got it." I sank my teeth into the ham, and such a lovely feeling went through me that, just for a moment, I forgot our plan and started munching.

"Durf, what are you doing? Stop demolishing that ham and bring it down here."

I came to my senses and jumped off the table, pulling the ham down with my teeth. It was so big and awkward that it fell out of my mouth and bounced on the floor. I dragged it across the kitchen while Zippo expertly nosed the back screen door open. Now this was what I called real teamwork. Then we ran out into the field, both of us lugging the ham along with our teeth until we stopped to chew at it and play with it. Zippo had been right: the crows in the trees started up a ferocious racket as soon as they saw us—hoarse, rowdy, and ear-splitting, and maddened beyond all reason. Perfect. Our plan was coming together like clockwork.

Suddenly, I felt my collar being forcefully grabbed and I heard those words, "You moronic mutt!" It was That Man, accompanied by Granny. I'd been so preoccupied with the taste and the fragrance and the fun that I hadn't even noticed them coming. Then the ham was torn from my mouth—rather rudely, I thought, until I realized that it was only Granny joining in our game.

I heard her saying, "I'll kill that blankety-blank yet." Zippo told me later she was talking about me. But I couldn't believe that. I didn't hear her words too clearly because of the racket from the crows. One of them had pitched on the ham and Granny knocked it off with her broom, so it must have been that crow she wanted to kill. No matter. It was the blankety-blank words that I really liked and wished I'd been called by that name.

Perhaps it was lucky I wasn't, though. I heard Nice Boy using one of those words, later, and Nice Woman responded, "Don't you ever let me hear you say that again."

"Why not? I heard Granny saying it."

"Granny? No. You couldn't have. When?"

"After Durf ran off with the ham that time, and then before that, when he jumped up on her lap and drenched her with wine."

"Oh. Well, that was different. Those were special circumstances. I think we can forgive her for that."

Anyway, at the country place on that day, which has since become known to history as "Durf and the Magnificent Baked Ham Caper," I heard that only Granny and That Man and Nice Boy knew before lunch about the fun Zippo and I had had with the ham. Everyone else was still on the lawn on the other side of the house. I heard talk later that there were some changes in the lunch proceedings. First, lunch was delayed by a good half-hour or more. Second, the menu was drastically altered. When all the invited guests were seated around the dining room table, Granny brought in a big bowl from the kitchen and announced, "Fettuccine Alfredo with ham."

One of the kids helping her said, "I thought we were having sliced ham and green peas and mashed potato and Dijon mustard, Granny. This ham is all diced up and covered in pasta and a thick creamy sauce."

Granny gave her a tight smile and a kiss and whispered, "I changed my mind, sweetheart, because this is even better."

Everyone tucked right into the meal, Zippo told me, except for

That Man. Despite the fact that he well knew the ham had been cleaned up and reheated to kill the germs, if any, he just pushed the small pieces of ham around his plate and only picked at the pasta. I didn't see any of this going on myself because, during what must have been a game of hide and seek after the ham was brought back in the house, I got accidentally barred in a back room. No one could find me until my family was ready to go home, and then That Man guided me by my collar right into our car so I wouldn't get lost again.

As I trotted along I heard all the guests telling Granny how delicious the meal was. So the day was highly successful for everyone, especially Granny. While she and Grampy were saying goodbye to the guests, she looked happy, if a little worn out by all the jollity. Zippo came out and barked at me, saying, "Next time you're here maybe she'll have a chicken cooked. That'll be easier for us to finish off than that big fat ham."

Granny picked him up, looked at me, and said, "Yes, bark at him, Zippo. Perhaps you'll bark a little bit of sense into him." Ha ha ha. I loved Granny and the fun we had bantering with each other.

What was I talking about? Oh yes, names. The end result was that it was too late to receive the name I liked from Granny's "blankety-blank" words or That Man's "Moronic Mutt." And come to think of it, Baked Ham would have been a good name, too. But I already had my real name by then, from my first day at our house when That Man, as would become usual, misunderstood me. See, when Nice Boy and Nice Girl asked me what I'd like to be called that day, my reply to their question was a little bark, which meant, obviously, "That's too important a question to think about on an empty stomach—I haven't eaten for at least half an hour, so let's eat first and decide on names afterwards."

But instead of responding to my reasonable request, That Man said to Nice Boy, "What did he say? Was it 'Urf' or something?"

Nice Boy said, "It sounded like 'Durf.'"

Everyone repeated "Durf" half a dozen times and agreed: Durf was an excellent name. Nice boy said to me, "What do you think, little doggy? Do you like Durf for a name?"

I barked, "Durf," meaning, again, "Let's eat first . . ." But "Durf" my name became. I soon realized how beautiful it sounded, though, when Nice Boy said, "Here, Durf, a doggy chew for you."

And talk about a mind-boggling coincidence later that day: Nice Boy told me, while he was lying on his back on the floor and I was sitting on his chest, that in the ancient Doggish language the name Durf meant "The very best pup in the whole wide world." He had looked it up in the Doggipedia, he said. So it had to be true.

Chapter 3

I Became a Dog Just in Time to Control the Cat Invasion

Yes, I know. Everyone called me a pup or a dog from day one—
"good pup," "nice doggy," "excellent puppy," and maybe even "bad
dog" once or twice. So how could I go on believing I was human
right into my teenage years? Because it never occurred to me they
meant I was really a dog, that's why. I thought they were using
cute little names on me, like other people did to their family
members and friends: "doll," "sweetheart," "honey." Sure, I heard
Nice Woman call That Man "sweetness and light" one time—go
figure that out! And I heard Granny whisper to Grampy that he
was a "real tiger" and she gave him a big kiss. A tiger? Grampy?
Just because Granny called him that? I think not. So why was I
supposed to be a dog or a pup just because people called me that?

I first came to my senses that I was not human, but something
else, the day our whole family made a trip to Terra Nova National
Park. We three kids—Nice Boy, Nice Girl, and I—sat in the back
seat the whole way, so by the time we arrived three hours later
we were full of energy. Right off the bat I bounced about the cabin,

yelping and whining, tugging at the leg of Nice Boy's jeans, pawing at the door, standing up on my hind legs at the window and nearly pulling the curtain off its rod and getting in the way of everyone unpacking. Even That Man picked up on my message: Durf was taking the family on a hike—and right now!

I ran out front, leading the way, and That Man walked right behind me. Sometimes I spotted a nice bog off to the side of the trail and headed for it to show everyone how we could all have fun jumping about in the mud and the waterlogged peat. But That Man would shout, "No, Durf, here. This way." And I'd run back, since he had his little heart set on it and I didn't want to spoil his holiday, and then I'd barge out in front once more to show the whole family that I was the real leader. Yes, back then I might have thought I was a human youth, but I was already developing superb top-dog instincts.

As we hiked, we came to this long, narrow boardwalk over a huge wide bog. Now, why the park people would put a wooden walkway over a lovely big bog like that was beyond me; I couldn't imagine anything better than traipsing, lunging, and slogging your way in the bog, up to your belly or higher in black mire and soggy turf, covered with that beautiful swampy smell. Only when I started trotting on the long, narrow boardwalk and saw it taper off into the distance, with two or three other boardwalks branching off it, did I understand why some genius had placed it here. It was perfect for running fast on. The sight of all those runways over the bog made me take off like a rocket. I felt as if I was superhuman. At least I did until this dog suddenly showed up out of nowhere, yellow-coloured and young and frisky.

"Oh, look at the beautiful golden retriever," said Nice Woman.

The sight of the dog trotting toward me in playful mode made me gallop even faster on the wooden boards. When he reached the runway he took off with me, both of us flat out, with our backsides down low and our hind legs reaching so far forward they went ahead of our front legs before thrusting backwards again. We whizzed by each other, we chased each other—I could feel the solid wood against my four paws, the air swishing past my ears; I could see the other retriever's ears flopping and trailing in the wind, his nostrils flaring, just like mine felt. No one in history ever ran as fast as I did that day . . . as both of us did. We were in control of the world.

I yipped and yelped at my family as I galloped, "Join in, come on, join in!" But all they did was stand there and laugh and clap their hands and cheer us on. That encouraged us to keep going, back and forth, pell-mell, helter-skelter, a mile a minute. Then I heard, above the wind and our paws on wood and our panting and the ruckus from my family, a voice in the distance, calling. Instantly, the golden retriever stopped in his tracks, twitched his ears up, and listened. Then he took off toward the path leading away from the runway and disappeared in the woods. We hadn't said a word to each other the whole while, but we understood each other perfectly.

I stopped, too, disappointed, of course, that he was gone, and looked at my family. Why didn't they join me in this best activity in the world? Then it came to me as I looked at the poor things standing there, pathetically upright on their two back legs: they couldn't! They simply could not gallop about as I and the golden retriever had been doing.

This was not the first time I'd noticed some defects in their nature. I'd asked myself before why they weren't able to pick up the magnificent smells that I was zeroing in on—a dog's markings on a pole down the street, a dead rat in a vacant lot three streets over, an upturned, oozing garbage can way down by the supermarket. And now here they were, not able to charge madly along the boardwalk with me and sail over the bog beneath.

I suddenly realized how completely different they were from me . . . and from my galloping partner. He and I were blessed with four great legs and paws for dashing, scampering, and darting like crazy on a boardwalk, and my family members weren't. It had never occurred to me before this that I was in any way the same as the dog Zippo. He and I did not seem to be similar at all. But the other retriever and I were very similar. Except for his longer fur, we were almost exactly the same. I was just like him and he was a dog, a superbly equipped dog. It came to me in a flash—my life-changing eureka moment—I too was a dog!

A sense of excellence arose in me. Everything was clear now. I trotted and pranced and strutted about the boardwalk proudly, until Nice Boy called out, walking toward the trail, "Come on, Durf. We're going back to the cabin for some chow," and I zoomed off the wood to rejoin them for our family supper.

From then on I was a proud dog, mostly. Oh, sure, sometimes, in my excitement with Nice Boy and Nice Girl it would slip my mind that I wasn't human like them and, for a little while, I would become a human kid again. This was especially true when it came to having a nap on a bed, or jumping up on a chair to take my meal from a plate full of food on the table, or standing up on my hind legs to hug a friend of the family with my front paws, before hearing that tedious, "No, Durf, down!" and that ungentle yank on my collar.

As my veterinarian told the family during one of my visits to her for some patching up, "With a people dog like Durf, his belief that he's human cannot be completely cured; you can only try to manage the condition."

Part of managing the human condition, so that I'd always be aware I was a dog, came with my education at doggy school later. That learning experience might not have ruined the instructor's life if every word out of his mouth hadn't been a determined attempt to browbeat me into doing what he wanted: "No, Durf," "Sit, Durf," "Down, Durf," "Stay, Durf." Would it have killed him just once to ask me to do something *I* wanted? "Eat, Durf," or, "Yes, Durf, by all means, do join the lady dogs." But I'm ahead of myself. We'll come to all that in its proper place, after I've bitten the bullet and introduced to my memoirs these two harrowing characters who now overran my house.

I was lucky I'd become a dog before it happened and was therefore ready and equipped with the strength and character to deal with the situation. Otherwise I would've been walked over by them and their so-called "cuteness," as badly as my human family was. Yes, I'm talking about those two cats who soon became, inexplicably, everyone's great buddies and who acted like they were rulers over everyone else in the place, in spite of the fact that everyone knows a dog is the natural boss in charge of cats. The two of them were forever sticking their noses into everything I was responsible for in the house and, to be honest, if it weren't for my leadership they would've had the total run of the place. As it was, they lorded it over the other family members something horrible.

Get your head around this shock to my system, if you can: I had just completed a patrol of the streets around our neighbourhood and was barking at our back door, expecting the normal top-dog welcome home, when my sniffers took in a very hostile odour I was familiar with from outside. Cat? Could one of the foolhardy critters have been actually hanging around *my* door? But after the door opened, the scent came, unbelievably, from *inside,* not out. My first thought was that I had to act fast; I had to clear the house of the unwelcome intruder. I was about to lunge in when That Man grabbed me by the collar. "We have to see how he reacts to them first," he said to Nice Woman and Nice Girl and Nice Boy, "before we let him go free."

See how I react? To a cat invading our house? That Man was dimmer than I thought. I strained at my collar to get at the trespasser, and gradually I pulled him into the kitchen. There I got the jolt of my life. Up in the arms of Nice Woman and Nice Girl were, not just one cat, but two. And they were being cuddled! Nice Girl said, "These pussycats are coming to live with us, now, Durfy. So you've got to be good friends with them." Caught between my strong urge to chase the two pests out of the house and being told by a beloved human that I had to be friends with them because they were here to stay, I was so stunned I went right weak and whiny. I collapsed to the floor and felt like I'd lost my will to live.

Supper perked me up enough to survive having to listen all night to Nice Girl and Nice Boy repeating how much they really loved those cats and how happy they were to have them here. But they were kids, after all. Harder to take was hearing the two seemingly mature adults in the house misuse words like "sweet" and "adorable" on them left, right, and centre. However, because my poor family was completely duped and fooled by the cats at this point, I decided not to put my foot down right away, but to go along with them, temporarily, until that coming day when the blinders would drop from everyone's vision, and they would see eye to eye with me on the true, diabolical nature of cats. Then it would be, "Hasta la vista, pussies."

Nice Girl owned the cats or belonged to the cats—I never got that clear in my mind. Both of them were mostly grown. One was a big, long-haired male from an animal shelter. His elderly owner, with no family, had suffered a stroke and couldn't look after him. The other was a small, female tabby from a horse stable that no longer wanted her.

I broke the brutal truth to both felines as soon as my family left me alone with them. It would take way more than the two of them together, I said, to equal one dog like me in importance around here. And I stated frankly that I doubted if even a dozen more cats like them would be able to do the trick.

The little female walked over to me, slowly. I figured she wanted to bow down before me. But she reached up and batted me across the chops with her paw. If I was expecting a tap of acknowledgement of my overlordship, or even gratitude for my tolerance of her as underling, that wasn't it. Those claws were out. I decided to tone down the formalities for the moment. "Hey, take it easy, spawn of a witch," I said. "I'm only joking."

"So am I only joking," said the little tabby. "And here's another jest." She clobbered me again, this time across the snout. "I hope you appreciate how well my sense of humour is working today." It made me sneeze, but I can assure you that smack didn't tickle. She raised her paw again, curved needles protruding, and asked, "What did you mean by spawn of a witch?"

"I have no idea," I said. "I heard it on TV during Halloween. They were talking about a cat. I didn't mean anything by it. I was just saying. It seemed to fit. You don't have to be violent all the time. In this house, under my leadership, if anyone mentions something you disagree with, we discuss it equally, until I lay down the law."

"I'm not keen on speechifying," she said. "I'm more into reacting violently. Especially when there's absolutely nothing you can do about it when I belt you across the schnozzle. Because if you hurt me our family will kill you. See the pickle you're in, you big dopey mutt?"

Suffice it to say I didn't deem my first meet-and-greet day with the little female cat a total success.

Meanwhile, the large male cat was sitting over there looking nonchalant and indifferent, although it was hard to tell what his mood was from his broad blue face, snub blue nose, and big yellow eyes. He was a fluffy blue Persian cat called Xerxes, which That Man said everyone had to learn to pronounce right: *zerkzeez*. Then, as usual, he threw another piece of useless info at the family: the original Xerxes was an ancient Persian king, and his name meant "ruling over heroes."

Our Xerxes, the Persian cat, was delighted with his name. It was completely appropriate for his exalted position in life, he said, if you considered a big oafish water dog and a scrawny little barn cat to be heroes worth ruling over.

At his mention of "scrawny little barn cat" I saw the female tabby moving stealthily toward Xerxes. I figured she meant to punish him as she'd done to me. But before she reached him, Xerxes concluded his remarks by saying that the important part of his name for everyone to keep foremost in mind all the time was the "ruling" part and to govern themselves accordingly.

That made the little female cat stop and snigger. Then she agreed that Xerxes was a perfect name for him because she'd heard Nice Girl and Nice Boy talking about King Xerxes after they looked up the name in the encyclopedia: the Persian King invaded ancient Greece with the biggest army and navy in the world and couldn't even defeat the tiny Greek army and navy, but got trounced by them. Then King Xerxes finished up his brilliant career by getting himself murdered by his own bodyguard. In other words, said the little female cat, he was a complete loser, so the name certainly did suit. "But don't worry," she told our Xerxes with an evil grin, "I'll make sure you're safe here, because I'm going to act as your bodyguard."

Xerxes replied, "That will not be required, thank you."

The little female cat was called Joey Smallwood. Either she came with the name or That Man was behind it. I heard him say that, in spite of her small size, she immediately started ordering around everybody in sight, just like the original Joey. He was right about that. Our Joey's favourite line of reasoning in any discussion, though, as she'd promised, was the clout across the nose with a paw.

Early on, I hid my jealousy when Nice Girl played with Joey, and I pretended to watch with enjoyment. The cat seized her sleeve in her front claws and then looked like she was trying to disconnect her hand from her wrist with about twenty quick thrusts of her hind paws. Nice Girl said that if little Joey were the size of a 300-pound tiger, that is, a hundred times bigger than she actually was, no other tiger, or even a lion, would stand a chance against her. I noticed, though, that Joey's claws, which were often "accidentally" out when she cuffed me, were always drawn in whenever she roughhoused with Nice Girl.

Joey, whom our refined Xerxes had called "a scrawny little barn cat," was . . . well, a scrawny little barn cat. Nice Girl had brought her home from the stable where she kept her Newfoundland pony. The little cat's mother was famous as the best rat catcher for miles around, and Joey was fast learning Mom's tricks of the trade when the stable decided to reduce their cat population. "I had to save her," said Nice Girl. "I couldn't just let them . . ." She didn't finish her thought but went quickly on with the notion that Joey was very cute and active from an early age and would be a great little buddy for Xerxes.

"Cute? A buddy? How can such a smart girl be so wrong on both counts?" Xerxes wondered. "Oh, I love Nice Girl and everything, but first of all, what's so cute about a kitten who was so ferocious when her own mother was nursing her out at the barn that the mother often had to jump up on a high windowsill just to get away from those needle-like teeth digging into her nipples?"

"I'm glad you heard about that," said Joey, yawning wide to show her sharp little fangs. "You can't say you weren't forewarned."

Xerxes moved farther away before saying, "And how could anyone think that a common tabby cat, with those very ordinary short-haired greyish stripes, could be a proper companion or, in the vulgar tongue, a 'buddy,' for King Xerxes, the gloriously long-haired blue Persian?"

"Didn't you hear That Man telling Nice Girl that the pattern on the fur of tabbies was known as 'grey tiger'?" asked Joey. "And that the beautiful design on our fur came from our direct ancestor, the African Wildcat? Well, you'll find out that those are good descriptions as time goes on, especially the 'tiger' and 'wildcat' parts."

I don't know if That Man was right about where Joey's fur came from. He was always yakking on with so much old hogwash about those cats that I often wished he would just button up. But I will say this. His "wildcat" description of Joey was dead-on. I first witnessed it the day she arrived, when she climbed the curtains at the windows and leaped from one shredded curtain to the next one. And I confirmed that she was definitely in the wildcat category our first Christmas together.

Joey climbed up the trunk of our Christmas tree at a mad dash and erupted from the top like a rocket blasting off and landed on all fours on the curtain hanging five feet away. During the dozen times I saw her doing it, she never knocked an ornament off the tree. But she made the branches shake to the point where the kids would grin at each other, when one of them saw her casually approach the tree, and whisper, "Earthquake alert."

Xerxes was a big disappointment to Joey in most cat activities, especially the tree-climbing department. Xerxes always stood back, pretending he was not transfixed in admiration at Joey's sprint up the trunk and her blast-off at the top. And he always responded to her urgings to join her by shrinking farther back and saying, "I'd love to. I really would. But I have too much respect for the Christmas tradition to taint it with vulgar activities. Besides, if I got that sticky sap all over my beautiful long fur it would break everyone's heart."

Christmas morning, Joey said to me, "That blue fluff ball over there is useless, so you'll have to climb the tree with me. It's no fun unless there's two doing it."

"Oh, I certainly will, Joey, when some wicked witch turns me into a stupid cat."

"You don't have to be a cat," Joey said. "Even a dumb dog can do it. And you don't have to do it fast like me. Climb nice and slow and you'll be able to slide in between the branches. Plus you don't have to leap off the top of the tree and land on the curtain the first time you do it."

The truth is that I was almost tempted. I was really envious of Joey's climbing skills, and I found it hard to admit to myself that she could do something that I couldn't. But, of course, I was far too intelligent to fall for her wily persuasion. Besides, I wanted my darn Christmas present.

Nice Boy and Nice Girl were over on the sofa with Nice Woman opening gifts. That Man was sitting on the floor, his back to the tree, with a pile of gifts in front of him. He was reading the labels on them and calling out names. Where the heck was mine? I sauntered over to the tree and sniffed at a few. That Man said, "Don't worry, Durf. I'll find yours in a minute."

With that, Joey sashayed by me. "Merry stupid Christmas, you big stunned St. John's sewer mutt," she said, whacking me on the nose right in the middle of a sniff. "You can't catch me." She took off for the tree trunk in a flash.

Well, that was it! I didn't care what the rule against the annihilation of cats was around here, she was getting it! I lunged under the tree and reared up, forcing my head between the lowest branches. Yes! I could do this! But the top of my head wouldn't seem to go through the gap. Unexpectedly, I found myself standing there with no tree over me. But I heard an ear-piercing roar from That Man and turned toward the sound.

I couldn't see much of him except for the slippers on his feet. The rest of him was covered by Christmas tree. I didn't know what had gone wrong, exactly, but something had. Instead of me climbing the upright tree as I'd intended, and nabbing that cat, the tree was lying across the living room floor and That Man was awkwardly crawling out from under it.

I looked at Nice Woman and the kids; maybe they could tell me what had just happened here. Their faces showed surprised and distressed expressions. But when That Man said, "I'm okay, no, no, I'm okay," and stood up with his hair, pajamas, and dressing gown covered in tinselly icicles and green needles from the fir tree—a big sparkly snowflake was dangling from one ear—I knew I had added to the family's Christmas joy. Because Nice Boy and Nice Girl started to titter and giggle, and although Nice Woman kept most of a grin off her face, I could see that she was struggling. That Man, on the other hand, was not tittering or grinning at all. He walked over to me without a word, grabbed me by the collar, and started to drag me out of the room.

Nice Boy and Nice Girl ran after us. "Dad, what are you *doing*?"

"What I'm doing is escorting this walking catastrophe out to the backyard."

"Dad," the kids cried, "this is Christmas!"

You'd think he would have already known that, with a Christmas tree falling on top of him. But it took their reminder to make him relent, and he grudgingly let me go. Even so, he gave me a dirty look every two minutes and grimly shook his head. He did that despite the fact that the whole family now had the extra fun of putting the tree up a second time and being able to decorate its branches again.

Besides, Nice Boy put his finger right on who was to blame for the tree toppling over in the first place: "Next Christmas we'll have to make sure that Durf gets his present first thing." He was too polite to come right out with it and state the obvious: That Man, the clueless gift delivery guy, was totally the author of his own misfortune.

Joey strutted over sporting a wide feline grin. Normally she was nearly as hard to please as That Man. But this morning she said that she really enjoyed my adventure. Something about the whole Christmas tree scenario, though, made me feel a little resentful of Joey. I had a nagging feeling that she was somehow responsible for That Man's mood swing against me. So I invented a mean insult: "Joey, I heard That Man saying that the 'M' in the fur on your forehead stands for the Monster from hell or the Misery from the black abyss."

Xerxes jumped in: "I never heard That Man saying any such a thing, Durf. Oh, your point is a good one, for sure—monster, misery—who could contradict that about Joey? But I believe you just told a fib."

Joey said to him, "You don't have to call the mutt a liar every time he gives me a compliment. Leave the big galoot alone, Herpes."

Herpes. That was what Joey had started to call our blue Persian: not Xerxes, but Herpes. She claimed that she had misheard his name when she'd first arrived. But when Xerxes straightened her out on the right pronunciation many times, she said she was sorry but the name Herpes had become so imprinted on her brain from her misunderstanding that she couldn't push it out. "Besides, admit it," she said, "Herpes suits you way better than that other foolish name, because it means you're going to be hanging around forever." And so, to our wild little tabby, our stately blue Persian remained Herpes eternally after.

I figured Joey had difficulty with my name, too, because she called me, not Durf, but Dork. I asked her, "Is Dork imprinted on your brain, too, like Herpes?"

"No," she said, "I know your real name is Durf."

"Then why do you call me Dork?"

"It's obvious," she said. "If you could see yourself as I see you, it would be *so* clear to you that, physically and mentally, the name that really works for you is Dork."

"The 'K' sound in a name makes it sound more impressive, right?" I said. "I heard that on television once about a commercial for K-9 Dog Chow."

"Yes, that's it, exactly. The 'K' sound in Dork makes you seem way more impressive." And so I became Dork to our tabby cat, and Dork I stayed. I have to say in all honesty that Joey could, when she made the effort, really inspire you with a good feeling about yourself.

This whole new name business got Xerxes thinking. He wanted to be helpful to Joey, he said. So he was going to alter her name from Joey to Jo-*ella* to remind her that she was in fact female and that she should therefore be gentle and feminine and, most important, completely obedient to Xerxes, as the superior tomcat on site.

Joey responded to Xerxes from over in the corner where she was busy stalking an ant. "Thanks for the help, Herpes," she said. "Come over here till I give you a nice, gentle, feminine hug and kiss." Delighted at the instant improvement he had effected in Joey, Xerxes lumbered over to her. Joey reached up with her paws, put them around Xerxes's neck, and touched noses. I was glad the rest of the family didn't see that, because I was well and truly sick of hearing them say how sweet those two were. Then Joey drew back and pasted Xerxes across the nose with her paw. "I hope that helps you, too."

"Ouch. That smarts, Joella," said Xerxes. "What do you mean, 'helps'? Helps with what?"

"Well, just like you're helping me by giving me the name Joella, I'm going to try as a friend to bring out the best in you, too. You're trying to make me more feminine, so I'm going to try to make you more like a real cat and less like a toy animal. Every chance I get I'm going to work on that snub nose of yours with the idea of making it swell up and get bigger and stick out more, like the nose on a true, authentic, macho tomcat."

"That will not be necessary," said Xerxes. "I can be sufficiently macho without a swollen nose."

"Hey, what are friends for?" So, whether Xerxes thought it necessary or not, Joey stuck to her game plan of improving her friend's nose with a good smack every chance she got.

"I see your point about Xerxes's nose," I said to her, "but what's your reason for batting me in the nose all the time, too, Joey? Don't you think my nose sticks out enough?"

"Enough? You've got the opposite problem, Dork. You're a St. John's sewer dog, so . . ."

"Water dog. A Labrador retrie—"

"Whatever. Your nose already sticks out way too much. My job is to improve you by making it a couple of inches shorter. That'll take time, so I'll work on it as often as I can. It would be a real drudgery if it weren't for this upside: you can't do anything about it. You have no idea how much fun it is for a cat to be able to bash a big dog in the snout without fear of revenge. Dorky, I love this place."

She was right. Knowing that we were one big happy family in this house meant that my job was to protect her along with everyone else, and never to hurt her. And besides, I didn't mind an "accidental" scratch from time to time. More than anything, though, I liked our little play-fights. They usually started by Joey making sure that at least one family member was watching, and then saying to me something like, "I don't understand why cats run away from dogs all the time. Take you, for example, Dork. You're about as scary as a cream puff."

That was my cue to have a fun-fight, and I'd rush over and pretend to bite her. Joey would pretend to be overpowered and lie on her back, grab my face in her front paws, and kick my chin fast about a hundred times with her back paws. I think she was a little prone, early on, to get overexcited, because she had no idea, with all our playing going on, how much that stung. So what I started doing in future "fights" was leading with my rear end.

That didn't sting nearly as much when Joey batted at it, or when she climbed up on my back and held herself steady there with her claws and her teeth. I'd twirl around and around snapping at her with my teeth, forcing myself to keep my distance, of course, and controlling my urge to really bite her because of the way the kids paid too much attention to the cats all the time.

Nice Girl and Nice Boy laughed at us. "Joey looks like she's trying to bring down a water buffalo," they said. After we entertained them with that for a while, I plopped down on my stomach for a rest, and Joey came and nudged at me with her head, to make sure I was simmered down and peaceful, she said. Then she lay down between my paws and started purring.

"Don't get the idea I like you or anything," she said once. "This is just a good place to cool down after the workout."

Everybody in the family said, "Awww, look. How cute. They certainly love each other."

"It's wonderful how we've got everyone fooled," Joey said.

Then Xerxes meowed, "Cute? You call that cute? This is cute." And he promenaded over to us and squeezed into the space left between my paws and plunked himself down beside Joey so that she was half smothered by Xerxes's excessive fur. Then both of them gently pawed at my mouth, sometimes hooking a claw in my lip, accidentally of course, and pulling it down so far the kids laughed again.

The kids often took pictures of the three of us there like that. I saw some of the snaps and was glad to see that I was lying there with my head held high, gazing off into the distance looking appropriately embarrassed by the presence of the cats between my paws. That meant I could explain to other dogs, if they ever saw one of those pictures, that it wasn't my fault. I had no choice: the whole family would be broken-hearted if I didn't go along with it. I never heard whether the snapshots won any prizes or not, but they should have.

Did I mention Xerxes's excessive, fluffy, blue fur? He had so much of it that he even had fur between his toes. Whenever Nice Girl or Nice Boy sketched a picture of Xerxes, they always wrote on the paper "furry between toes" and drew arrows pointing at his paws. That was cool, I must say. Mind you, I was very proud of my own webbed toes, but they would have been even better if they had fur between them, too. I didn't envy much about Xerxes, but I sure was jealous of that fur between his toes. I wouldn't say anything to him about it, though, because Xerxes was high and mighty enough already.

Joey never mentioned the fur between Xerxes's toes, either, but sometimes I saw her, when she thought no one was looking, gazing longingly at those paws. If Xerxes ever caught her eyeing them before she could glance away, he'd raise a paw in the air and spread his toes and gaze at the fur from every angle for a while with a very superior look, before bringing the paw to his mouth and thoroughly licking the fur between his toes. Often, Joey stood up and pretended to stretch casually, and coolly strutted from the room. I sometimes wondered what trouble and strife Joey's jealousy and Xerxes's flaunting of the fur between his toes was going to lead to. I would find out, much later. When I least expected it.

Chapter 4

Dog Academy

I felt lonely when Nice Boy and Nice Girl went off to school every day and Nice Woman and That Man went to work. Hanging around with two cats provided limited entertainment. I never did get the hang of that scratching post. And who would touch anything with a name like *cat*nip? When Joey did talk me into eating some one day, she said afterwards, "We won't give him any more of that, Herpes; it only made him dopier." I snuck out of the house whenever I could, but still, there were long hours of daily idleness, waiting, waiting, waiting for the absolute bliss when the kids got home.

What I really wanted to do was go to school with Nice Boy. One morning, when he got the bus to school, I barged out the back door behind him, ran down the driveway, and hopped aboard the bus with him. The kids all shouted, "Let him stay," and, "Bring him to school," but the driver made Nice Boy take me back to the house. Grown-ups!

I'd made my point, though. When Nice Boy got home that afternoon he told me that, unfortunately, his own school was already filled up with kids, but he was going to talk to his dad about me going to a school of my own. It would be a shame for a smart dog like me to let such a big brain go to waste, he said, so my higher education was an absolute must.

That night Nice Boy and That Man had an argument upstairs. I don't know what they were disagreeing about, but I heard That Man say as he left his son's room, "We can do it ourselves."

Next day, when That Man got home from work, he and Nice Boy and I went out in the backyard to play a game called "Durf's obedience training." This is the way the game worked—I think I have the rules right—if That Man said a certain word, like, say, "sit" or "stay" or "no," then I'd take off in a crazy zigzag gallop around the yard. Nice Boy liked the game, judging by the way he laughed. But That Man couldn't seem to get the knack of it, and the face on him showed no enjoyment. His seriousness kind of spoiled the game for Nice Boy, too, because, after a few growls—from That Man, not me—I could see my buddy starting to hide his amusement behind his hand.

The day after that, we played the game again. That Man was saying "sit" over and over and pressing my rear end down, monotonously, when I added to our fun by bulldozing myself headfirst between his legs, toppling him over onto the grass on his backside. I don't know why he yelled at me as he rubbed his bottom—I didn't hide that rock in the grass. Then he hobbled back into the house muttering to Nice Boy, "Okay, that's it, you're right," and got on the phone.

The next night, Nice Boy and his dad finally brought me to a proper school, too. It was just like his, Nice Boy said, and I went there regularly, three nights a week. Until, that is, the troubles arose, and the instructor lost his grip on reality.

Dog Academy was the cool name they had on the place, and "Training for Respect and Awareness" was their mission statement. That jibed precisely with my plans, because I intended to set myself up as the ringleader of the other students, so that their awareness and respect of me was foremost. But what a shock I got when I went in and cased the joint on my first night. By then I had already developed street smarts by roaming about the town and hobnobbing with dogs of mixed and varied types. But the dogs at the school were mostly the hoity-toity kind, which, I was surprised to learn from the instructor, I was assumed to be, too; we were expected to be doing our breeds proud.

Every kind of a specimen known to dogdom was present: little round fluffy ones not as big as ducks, let alone able to swim out and bring a duck back in; tall dogs with weird haircuts; thick burly dogs with strange fur patterns and colours . . . and they were all totally full of themselves. I couldn't count the times I heard a dog say, in a plummy accent, something like, "My dear, that one over there has her greedy little heart set on winning Best in Show, but I've got other plans."

At first it was a bit intimidating and I stayed close to Nice Boy. But after about ten minutes, I was used to all the appearances and the smells, and I realized that the girl dogs, at least, even the bizarre ones, looked really lovely to sniff and impress, especially the one who whispered to me that Durf was a handsome name for a handsome lad. So, naturally I wanted to make friends.

The instructor had different ideas. He was turning out to be a bigger control freak than That Man, which, I'm sure, no one thought possible. He had it in his head that, instead of playing my catch-me-if-you-can game after he said "sit," "stay," "down," "come," and "heel," I should actually do what the words said. Talk about a waste of time, because I'd known how to do all those things from the day I was born.

Whenever I'd felt like it, I sat and stayed, and I flopped down, right on my stomach, if the urge came over me. And I knew how to come to Nice Boy every time he filled my feeding dish or even opened the fridge door—no big deal. He didn't even have to ask—I could be upstairs, and still I'd come whenever I heard the sounds. And as for "heel," I already knew how to grab That Man's or Nice Boy's pants cuff behind the heel with my teeth, for fun, and hold on for dear life. If anything I was too good at that, judging by That Man's reactions whenever he shook and pried me loose and told me to stop it. So what was I expected to do here in school, anyway—"heel," as the instructor said, or "not heel," as That Man demanded? This was becoming unnerving. Didn't Pavlov's dog suffer a nervous breakdown from indecision induced by conflicting stimuli? Nice Boy had already warned me about that months ago when he saw me one time hovering between licking Joey and biting her. I rest my case.

But still, this instructor at the school kept saying, "Those are the five basic commands that every dog must learn to obey." You heard right: to add insult to injury, I was supposed to "obey" all that old stuff whenever he wanted me to. It made no sense. Why on earth would he want me to sit or stay for no reason as I stood in the middle of a gymnasium floor surrounded by dogs who just wanted to have fun? Honestly, what was wrong with this guy?

When I got back home that night, Joey said, "Cats are too well behaved to need an obedience school, so I've never been to one. What was it like? Fill me in."

I described my long minutes of intensive training to her, and this weird concept of commands. "Commands?" she said. "Where the heck were you? In a war zone somewhere? Oh, I get it. You're training to be a soldier. Did they teach you how to salute yet?"

"Salute? What's that?"

"This." Joey sat on her haunches and raised a paw up to the side of her head. I sat back and tried it, too. I had trouble doing it as smoothly as Joey. My paw came up from the front rather than the side, and I clunked myself in the eye with it. And it wouldn't stay up unless I lowered my head and pawed the side of my face and snout, as if I were removing cobwebs. "That's pathetic," said Joey. "Even Herpes can do better than that. Salute for him, Herp, just like I did."

Xerxes got up on his haunches and raised his paw to the side of his head. "And look how cute he is," said Joey, "with those blue pads on his paws and the fur between his toes. He may not look like a soldier, but he certainly puts you to shame with his great salute, Dork. We should send Herpes to that military school instead of you."

"Wait now," I said, "I don't think the instructor is even asking us to salute there."

"That'll come in the next class for sure. Any female dogs there, Dorky?"

"Yes, some really beautiful, exotic ones. There's one I'm head over heels in love with, my soulmate for life, and four more I'm developing a crush on. And I haven't even had a chance to sniff them all yet."

"Well, get your salute ready, my friend, so you don't make a total boob of yourself in front of all your sweethearts at the next class. This is more urgent than I thought. You'll need to practise all day tomorrow and the day after for the next session."

"Thanks for the heads-up, Joey old buddy, that's what I'll do."

Next day, when Nice Boy came home from school, I greeted him by practising my salute. "What's wrong, Durf?" he said. "Are your ears bothering you?" He looked in my ears and sniffed at them. "They seem okay. But we might have to bring you to the vet to see if you have an infection. She said Labs often have problems with their floppy ears and sometimes need surgery."

Surgery? The other night at school, a cocker spaniel with floppy ears told me that he went to the vet to have his ears operated on, or so his people said, but whatever they did to him there, he could hardly walk for a week. Needless to say, after Nice Boy mentioned surgery I only practised my salute when there was no one around.

The next night at the military academy, though, I brought my perfected salute into full play. The instructor was demonstrating the command "stay" and happened to be using me as his model. "Worst-case scenario," he said. While all the other dogs were parked on their rear ends doing nothing, I figured this would be a good time to show my salute to some of the lady dogs. I loped gallantly over to where two of them were sitting. The instructor approved because he let go of my leash, although he would claim later that I tugged it out of his hand. Over by the girls, I brought my paw up smartly to the side of my head, only slightly hurting my eye.

"Your lab is very defiant," the instructor said to Nice Boy in a miffed voice, coming over to me. "And what's he doing that with his paw for? Has he got ear mites?"

"I couldn't see any when I looked," said Nice Boy. The instructor pulled me back by the leash over the hardwood floor without so much as a "by-your-leave." Respect and Awareness? Contempt and Ignorance was more like it!

Next the instructor started to demonstrate the military command "down." He was still using me as his prize demonstrator—to stress the point, he said, that any dog, however rowdy and disruptive, could be trained. I bided my time for an opportunity to bolt over there and continue a display of my saluting skill to the females. It was imperative that I impress them. I had no choice. They were pretending to play hard to get, some even going so far as to turn away abruptly when I had earlier sniffed them in the friendliest way possible.

While the instructor was making everyone numb with boredom, describing how the command "down" was supposed to work, I saw out of the corner of my eye that he wasn't paying much attention to me right now. I took off. This time he couldn't claim I yanked the leash out of his hand, because he had it wrapped around his wrist. Instead, he had the fun of being dragged along the floor, skidding on the soles of his shoes.

He brought me to a stop about halfway over to the females. There, he said to Nice Boy, "Labs are smart, but they remain adolescent much longer than most other dogs, and some even pretend to be slow learners so that they can get their own way more." All very interesting, to exaggerate wildly, but those allegations of his were old hat to me.

Weeks ago, Joey and Xerxes had convened a special meeting between the two of them, with me as a guest observer, to try to figure out what ailed my brain. They had observed, they said, that whereas they had both gone from kittens to mature, sensible cats fairly quickly, it was taking me an awfully long time to become an adult dog, especially in the common-sense department. My body seemed adult, but my mind stayed very puppyish, said Joey, "and I don't mean 'puppyish' in the cute way." It was as if I was going to remain a teenager forever, she grumbled. The bigger and stronger my body got, the dafter and more infuriating my mind became: an everlasting, non-ending adolescence. For example, Joey asked, when was the last time I'd licked my fur clean?

I replied that I was sure I'd done it recently, "But, hey, don't ask me for a precise month. I'm not fanatical about it like you guys."

Then she ranted that I was always digging great big dirty holes out in the backyard, with all the earth flicking up on my belly and back legs and staying there, and that I brought big gobs of mud into the house and never bothered cleaning my paws, and that I made them jealous by drinking fresh, cool water out of the toilet bowl just because I could, while they were restricted to the warm water in their dishes, and that I chewed on everything in sight, drooling all over the carpet or couch or wherever I happened to be flopped down, and that I did my business out in the backyard or on the sidewalk without covering it up, forcing another family member to pick it up in a bag . . . Joey drew a deep breath. "There's lots more, but for now just face it, Dorky, you're a slob. And what's worse, a juvenile slob in an adult slob's body."

Xerxes chimed in: "So here we are, Durf, two cats who are as sensible as the day is long, and there you are, older than us but still unruly, goofy, undisciplined, unmanageable, never listen to reason, and—"

"Don't forget 'nuts,'" said Joey.

"Right. Thanks, Joella. And you're nearly always covered in some filthy goop of unidentified origin. So the question is, Durf, what are we going to do about it?"

"Do about what?" I asked. "What the heck is this 'it' you're bellyaching about?" I would have loved to help those guys, but I failed to grasp their problem.

So, tonight at the school, I wasn't hearing anything new from the instructor's allegation that I had the mental state of a mid-life adolescent. Plus, could he not clearly see that what he was babbling on about had absolutely no relevance to the reality of the situation, namely that a lady Dalmatian over there was giving me the eye?

"Durf, down!" he said again. Was this chap never going to stop boring everyone to death? To give the students a little break, I decided to trot over to make her acquaintance.

"I said DOWN!" roared the instructor and yanked on my leash. Hard. As hard as he could, judging by the sensation in my neck. I spun around and around on the hardwood floor, dazed and strangled by the well-named choke chain. Then there was a terrific pain in the back of my head, and the last image I saw before collapsing on the floor was the bluish face of the drill-sergeant instructor above me threatening to explode in rage.

My next memory was of That Man and the instructor laying me in the back seat of our car, where Nice Boy put his arms around me. I heard the instructor say, "I'm really sorry about that. Labs are so stubborn that I'm afraid I lost it a little in there."

"A little?" said That Man. "Buddy, the Puppy Whisperer you ain't."

At the pet hospital, the vet greeted me with her friendly welcome. "Back again, are we, Durf?" We were buddies from the patchwork she did on me now and then after some mishap during my exploration of the streets. Tonight, she told us that my neck was strained or sprained, but luckily no vertebrae were injured, and a little rest and medicine should fix me up. Meanwhile, I had to wear this brace contraption around my neck.

When I got home Joey said, "Dork! What's that collar thingy

on your neck? Did the military school send you off to war? Did you get wounded?"

"No, I got my injury when the instructor stopped me from trying to salute the girls and stuff." I saw an unfamiliar look of guilt creep over Joey's face.

"Joella, you ought to be well and truly ashamed of yourself," said Xerxes, "for the way you talked poor Durf into that silly salute to the other students. And you only did it because you were jealous he was climbing his way to the top by going to school." For once Joey didn't have a comeback. She even looked a bit sheepish.

The painkillers must have blunted my edge. "It wasn't all Joey's fault, Xerky," I said. "The instructor got mad at me because I wouldn't follow one of his commands."

"He maimed you just short of death because you wouldn't follow a command?" said Joey. "What command could that possibly be? It must have been a complicated one."

"It was 'down.'"

"Down? You mean you weren't able to follow the command 'down'? What did you think he meant by it? Sideways? Or, up? Herpes, you and I should give thanks daily that we were not born dogs and therefore we don't get confused between down and sideways and up. Ah, Dorky? Maybe you're not cut out for the soldier's life. Maybe you should leave that to the Doberman pinschers, German shepherds, and pit bulls. Then you can stick to the tomfoolery and crazy young love that you're really good at."

"You're making a lot of sense, Joey," I said.

"You going back to that military boot camp?"

"That Man says no. The instructor resigned. Nice Boy and his dad are going to home-school me again."

"Oh, great," said Xerxes. "We can kiss sanity goodbye again around here for a good while."

"He won't be that bad, Xerks," I said. "Nice Boy and I will keep That Man in line."

Xerxes and Joey turned to each other with looks of amazement for some reason, and slowly shook their heads.

Chapter 5

My First Near-Death Experience

In fact, I had more of an uphill battle than I expected, trying to manage and direct That Man properly. One evening when he and Nice Woman invited guests for dinner, he asked me to stay out of the dining room! I loved That Man dearly, but he definitely had control issues when it came to me. The cats were allowed to wander around the room to their heart's content. They didn't go in—they stayed in the living room or upstairs—but that's not the point; it was the principle of the thing. Therefore, when he wasn't looking and was full of himself telling some yarn to his table of captive audience, I went right in and strolled up to one of the diners who had been admiring me earlier.

I placed my chin on the table next to her plate of delicious poached salmon. I just loved Nice Woman's cooking. The guest said, with a lovely smile at me, "I do believe our sweet little Lab wants some of my salmon." Talk about quick on the uptake. She pushed her plate away from my nose, but lured by the mouth-watering smells, I reared up, put my front paws on her lap, and reached my snout in toward her plate.

"Durf," That Man growled, "down." He came around and took me by the collar. "Out," he said, and practically dragged me from the room and pointed at the mat by the cold, drafty front door. I lay there for a little while so as not to embarrass him in front of his guests by taking over control of the situation again right away. Then I crept over and eased myself down on the floor with my nose just outside the dining room door. The guests didn't say anything, but I could see from their smiles and glances aimed my way that they were yearning for me to come back in.

"We'd better not look at him," said That Man, unable to cover up his jealousy.

Gradually, at a very slow crawl on my belly, I inched my way back into the dining room. A tiger stalking its prey couldn't have done it better. Finally, after about a half-hour, I was all the way into the room again, and everyone was laughing in admiration at how sneakily I had slithered my way back in. One woman said, "Labs are great, aren't they?" Even That Man, who was not lacking a ruthless streak, didn't dare contradict such intelligence.

"All right, Durf," he had to say. "Stay down and be good."

Just then, the same woman stood up from the table and said, "Excuse me while I powder my nose before I tuck into that." At her place at the table stood a plate of what I was smelling—"Mom's world-famous chocolate mousse." That's what the kids called it, and they were right. They'd given me a full bowl of it to sample one time, and there could be nothing on earth more delicious. The woman who owned the plate of mousse that I was eyeing tonight smiled down at me as she walked from the room and said, "Sweet pup." A sure and certain invitation! And I didn't need to be asked twice. Up I lunged on her chair, swallowed most of the mousse in one gulp, and cleaned her plate in two more solid licks.

Some sixth sense had told me I had to act fast like that, and a good thing, too, because I was barely finished when That Man decided, in a voice too loud and with a tug on my collar much harder than necessary, that I should spend the rest of the evening out in the backyard.

"And no barking. Durf, don't make me come out here again."

It was starting to become clear to me that a showdown was looming between me and That Man. A few days after the dinner party, when I was left in the house again, all alone with two tiresome cats while everyone else went to school or their offices, I got an idea to make sure he knew who he was dealing with here. I went to every bedroom and bathroom, tipping over every hamper I could see, and rooted out all the dirty laundry. Then I strewed underwear and socks and shirts and sheets and towels all around the house, upstairs and down. I covered nearly every square inch of the floors and stairs. Even Joey was impressed. "Good job, Durf," she said, with a nice grin of appreciation at Xerxes.

I gnawed on some of the laundry. The socks were good and tasty, but not chewy enough to suit me. I went searching in That Man's closet for something more solid on the teeth. Of all the shoes there, the really shiny black ones appealed to me most. I picked them and went to work.

When everyone got home that evening, I figured That Man would be a little bit mad. That was the whole idea, after all. But for him to shout that he was going to buy a doghouse and put it out in the backyard and that I would be spending the rest of my days and nights out there? All because of his stupid old shiny shoes? Sure, he hardly ever wore that pair, anyway. I only saw them on his feet once, that time he dressed himself up like a penguin with a bow tie. He already looked as silly as could be in that fit-out, anyway, so what was the big deal if his precious shiny shoes had a few teeth marks on them?

The next morning, before everyone went to school and work, That Man had a chat with Nice Woman about what to do with me today "to prevent the total destruction of the house and everything in it." Does anyone else find that That Man's comedy act misses the mark? They decided, because of a protest from the kids, that I couldn't be left out in the backyard in such cold, wet weather. So I was to be jailed in the kitchen all morning with the doors sealed. Meanwhile, the cats would have the run of all the rest of the house, with their water bowls and Kitty Litter transported out there for the convenience of their highnesses.

When everyone had left, I didn't give up in despair. I bravely made the best of my predicament by scouring the table and counters and floor for evidence of food—dropped morsels, unswept-up crumbs, a plate with a remnant of butter and jam, a driblet of milk, a speck of sugar . . . something, anything! There was nothing. I could not believe my nose. Could That Man be so cruel as to deliberately assassinate me with hunger during that long haul between breakfast and the next meal? I ran to the door to the hall. "Joey, Xerxes, help me," I whined at it hysterically. "He's starving me to death."

"Oh, stop your snivelling, Dork," said Joey, "ya big sooky baby. You should have hidden away a piece of steak like I did . . . mmm."

"And I'll thank you not to wake me up from my nap every two minutes all morning with your blubbering," said Xerxes.

It was a toss-up who was more heartless, the barn cat or the aristocrat.

My vet had told my family before this that I seemed well-adjusted and free of neurosis. But she'd obviously never spent minutes alone in a barred and bolted kitchen. Because every neurosis on that afternoon doctor show I once watched, when That Man was home sick one day, welled up in me now: abandonment anxiety, locked-in syndrome phobia, searing realization that everyone in the world had stopped loving me, foreboding about why I, me, this subjective self, had emerged in this cruel universe. Why? Why? Why? I collapsed on the floor in existential angst.

I was close to the wall and the wallpaper was the only thing I could see, with its bright colours of flowers and leaves and clouds and sky. Nice Woman liked it very much, and I'd heard visitors praise it for livening up the kitchen. Before my eyes, down near the floor just above the baseboard, I noticed the small corner of wallpaper that had come loose. Nice Woman had spotted it last night, and That Man had undertaken to glue it back firmly to the wall "first chance." But of course, being all talk and no action around the house at the best of times, he hadn't done it. He and he alone had failed to make that repair. So there's no way around the fact that he was entirely to blame for what now took place in the kitchen that morning.

I stood up and took hold of the small, loose piece of wallpaper with my front teeth and pulled. Lo and behold, a good-sized swath came away from the wall. I yanked on that with all my might and weight and a big wide long strip tore off the wall and fell to the floor. Without my realizing it, the morning flew by.

By the time Nice Woman and That Man came home at lunchtime to see how we "little darlings" were making out, all the wallpaper in the kitchen, up to the level of my full height on my hind legs, was lying in pieces, big and small, across the kitchen floor.

Judging by their heartfelt reaction to that spectacle, you'd think Nice Woman and That Man would have learned their lesson for good. I mean to say, the moral to the story wasn't rocket science: *Do not imprison Durf in the kitchen ever again!*

Yet, a little while later I found myself, unbelievably, barricaded in there once more. The hall had just been freshly painted, was That Man's feeble excuse, and the cats even had to be farmed out to friends for the day. But I'd only gotten paint on me once before—that time the ladder out by the house, with the paint can on it, tipped over on me without explanation. And what was the big ruckus, then, anyway? The royal blue went so well with my yellow coat that even That Man said I should hire myself out as the Swedish flag. Yet here I was, now, caged in the kitchen alone again, being suffocated by paint fumes from the hall, while everyone else with a life went out to a day of fun in their offices and classrooms.

I was about to collapse on my blanket and have a nap of despair when it suddenly hit me that my nose was taking in some very beautiful whiffs besides the paint. I sniffed them to their source and spotted it—a great big book lying on the counter, its pages spread open. This had to be investigated. I pawed the book down to the floor and nosed its pages apart.

Page after page of photographs of the most mouth-watering food I'd ever seen sprang to my eyes. It was the book of recipes I'd often noticed Nice Woman looking at as she cooked. But, even better than the beautiful pictures, the odours from the pages were conjuring up scrumptious visions in my brain. I snuffled and snorted at the pages, zeroing in . . . heavenly! The fabulous smells were coming from the little stains that were speckled all over each page, scents that ranged from lamb to beef to codfish to lobster to bouillabaisse to chocolate mousse to . . . the list was infinite in scope and quality. The meaning of life opened up to me: I had been created to lick those pages. I couldn't help it. I don't remember much after that because I went into some sort of a zone in my head where I forgot about everything else except that I was in canine nirvana eating for eternity the meat and fish and desserts of which the pictures and fragrances coincided on each page.

I came back to reality when, dying of thirst, I seemed to drop from heaven to the kitchen floor. I noticed that the only thing left in front of me from the feast was a pair of gnawed and chomped book covers. The pages had vanished. I staggered over to my big bowl full of water and drank it all without stopping. I now felt so bloated I could not stand up. All I wanted to do was collapse and go unconscious. I flopped down and went out so cold that I didn't even hear Nice Woman and That Man coming in the door. I only heard right above me, though it sounded like it was far off in the distance, her voice saying, "Oh no, he ate my favourite book of recipes!" I tried to agree with her that it was certainly a book to love and cherish, but I could hardly lift my head an inch off the floor, and wagging my tail had become so hard to do, I could manage only a few twitches.

The next thing I remembered was lying on a table, where I could hear a woman and a man and see a flash of white coats, as they poked and prodded me and forced a tube down my throat, muttering, "Could be terminal bloat," and, "It may be too late . . . mightn't be able to save him." It was my vet and her assistant. Then later, as I awoke from a dream in which I'd come back through a long tunnel from the bright, warm, welcoming light at its end, I heard my vet saying to That Man and Nice Woman, "Miraculous. We didn't expect him to survive that. He must have the constitution of an ox."

That Man joked in his joy at my recovery, "Stunned as an ox, too."

"I'd say that's fairly accurate," said my friend, the vet. "So you'd better hide smelly cookbooks away from him from now on." Oh, good, I thought, emerging from my grogginess, she was suggesting a new game for us to play: find the yummy cookbooks.

That Man asked her, "Are you actually saying that, after what he just went through, he might be asinine enough to do this again?"

To which the vet replied, patting my chest lovingly, "Yes, I'm afraid that's exactly what I'm saying." I thought, darn tootin' I was asin . . . —whatever that word was—enough to do it again. I adored this woman. She understood me. Even when she'd given me my needles I didn't bark, howl, or whine at the jabs; I only whimpered.

The next day, when Xerxes and Joey came back to the house, I told them all about my visit to the pet hospital, dying of bloat, and asked them, "Does anyone know what 'asinine' means?"

Joey said, "Yes, I do, Dork. It means 'the very smartest that any dog can possibly be.'" I was beginning to warm to Joey. For a cat, she sometimes got things right. I gave her head a little lick of thanks. She ducked her head and batted me across the jaw, just to tease.

But then she had to go and spoil the mood by starting this conversation with Xerxes: "Listening to Dork talking about the hospital, Herpes, reminds me of something important. For the good of all animals and humans alike, we've got to get that dog fixed."

Chapter 6

Sweet-Looking Cats Can Be Really Diabolical

That sounded like it was going to be one of those cat conversations I didn't like the drift of. So I walked across the room, flopped down, and closed my eyes, pretending to go asleep.

"What do you mean fixed?" asked Xerxes. "I didn't even know Durf was broken."

Joey sighed. "Not fixed like that, Herpes. There's no way of fixing everything that's wrong with Dork. What I mean is altered—improved, like you were."

"What? I don't remember anything being wrong with me that had to be improved."

"Herpes, you're joking, right?" She waited for a response, and when Xerxes reacted with his normal blank look, she asked, "Do you even know what I'm talking about?"

"Yes, I know what you're talking about," said Xerxes in a huff. He took a moment to look himself over. "I think. Just remind me again, though. How did they improve me?"

"Don't you remember your human nearly starving you to

death one night and then bringing you to that pet hospital the next morning when you were about six months old?"

"Oh yes, now I remember, the nice place where they wore white coats like Durf was just talking about? I really enjoyed that holiday. I had a lovely nap there. I didn't even mind the dog yapping in the next room."

"You had a lovely nap and didn't mind the dog because they put a thingy over your head and zonked you out so that they could go to work and improve you."

"Zonked me out? Was that what was so good? I'd love to go there and do that again."

"One little dose of anaesthetic and he's already addicted to it," said Joey. "There's strength of character for you."

"Well, whatever they did to improve me, Joella, they did a really good job. Look how beautiful I am."

If Joey could have thrown her paws high and wide over her head in a gesture of despair, as our adult humans seemed to like doing with their hands at me, I'm sure she would have. "The point is not how beautiful you are," she said, "although I must confess you do sometimes look rather handsome in an effete, decadent, overly refined, and manufactured-blue-toy sort of way."

"That sounds really good, Joella. Thank you for the compliment. Where did you learn all those hard words?"

"I heard That Man say them about you one time. Every word a compliment. But never mind all that. The point is that you were altered and so was I. You were in and out of the hospital in jig time. But I had to stay there overnight. Just another example of the unfair treatment that exists between male and female cats."

"You sound resentful, Joella. Is that why you get mad at

me sometimes, because I'm a superior male on top of being so gorgeous compared to you?"

"You may be on to something, Herps. Let's see." She went over and rapped Xerxes across the cheek with her paw. "Yes, I was feeling a little mad at your male superiority and beauty before I did that, and now I feel much better."

"Oh, thanks for the opportunity to help," said Xerxes, just oozing sarcasm.

"You're welcome. The point I was making is that you and I were both improved, and that's what makes us such fine pets, all civilized and everything, compared to Dork over there."

Hearing Joey calling herself civilized, I couldn't help it: I had to let out a snigger. I hoped she would think it was one of my sleeping snorts. I snuck a look under my eyelids, and I didn't like the way she was eyeing me, coolly but, at the same time, suspiciously.

"And the reason why Dork is not civilized like us," Joey went on, "is that he has not been altered. And nobody can figure out why he's not. The dark truth of the matter is that, if any dog needed to be improved for the sake of peace and order in the world, it's our Dorky. So, Herpes, you and I need to do something about that. We've got to convince our humans that it must be done."

Joey was right about me not having been "improved" like them. I'd heard my humans discussing it when I was just a pup. They were talking about what superb specimens of Labrador retriever both my mother and my father were, and how they'd won prizes at dog shows, and that I was slated for dog shows, too, and when I won big prizes, I could be bred and produce other winners like me. If I was neutered, they said, I wouldn't be able to compete for Best in Show, because then I wouldn't be breeding stock. Therefore, they didn't have it done, and when I grew up I heard That Man joking to Nice Woman that not having me done was the biggest blunder they had ever made in their entire lives.

But how could that possibly have been a blunder? Well, according to That Man's idea of an explanation, the bigger I grew, the more my tail developed a twist or kink in it. My tail, he said, should have been straight and sleek like an otter's tail. But partway down its length, it twirled off to the right in a kind of half-curl. It looked great to me—perfectly lovely—but That Man brought me to some guy who called himself a "dog expert," and he said there was no way I should compete in a show because I'd be laughed out of the place. And it would also be a disgrace, he prattled on, if I were to pass on that dreadful defect to others in the Labrador retriever breed.

"Dog expert," did he call himself? I'd like him to repeat that twaddle about my dreadful defect to the lady dogs in our neighbourhood, every one of whom lavished friendship and affection on me without ever once mentioning my tail, except to praise it. And if anyone should know what a good handsome tail on a male dog is, a female dog should. The same goes for Nice Boy.

When I got home from this "expert," and That Man was telling the family what he'd said, Nice Boy hugged me and whispered, "I don't care what they say about your tail, Durfy. I still love you just as much." So my reply to "dog experts" everywhere is this: Pardon me all to heck if my tail didn't grow up to fulfill the superb promise you demand of tails in your nitpicking rule book! As if keeping those guys impressed were a big deal compared to that gorgeous lady bulldog three streets over.

The end result of that huge drama was that, because of my age, I had been left unimproved. Joey now called that a tragedy, mainly because of what she described as "the secret lives of wayward dogs." Here was one of her wild speculations: "I've seen an awful lot of stray dogs out there on the streets, Herpes, with the same kink in their tails that Dork has."

Those were the days when dogs of all kinds had the run of the town. Wherever you went outside, there were masterless mutts loping along the sidewalk or helping with the removal of garbage outside people's houses. And the more I considered Joey's words, the more I could visualize many of the younger dogs of all sizes— big ones, little ones, and everything in between—with tails at half-mast containing charming little twists in them.

I hadn't realized before Joey brought it to our attention how much the other dogs wanted to use me as their role model. It was flattering, but I honestly couldn't take any credit or blame for the fad. If I had established a fashion in tails, it was obviously because the younger ones all wanted to be cool like me: that was their choice, not mine. I couldn't resist lifting my head and telling Joey exactly that, now.

She snorted in what sounded like derision and said, "Okay, we'll have to forget about all the weird Dorky dog tails everywhere you look. Explaining that to you guys would be just too much of a challenge. So let's talk about the time Dork, in his wild, unimproved state, nearly killed the mailman. Remember that, Herpes?"

"Most regrettably, I do," said Xerxes, nodding sadly at the memory.

But that was pure exaggeration by Joey. Why would I want to kill the mailman who was always full of praise for me? One day, when he was dropping off his letters, I heard him say to Nice Boy, "That's quite a dog you've got there. He's really good at shedding his fur. Coming down the sidewalk just then, I saw yellow fur blowing around like tumbleweeds in a western movie."

Nice Boy said, "My Dad says a sandstorm in the Sahara Desert has nothing on Durf's fur storms. And we can't figure out why his fur sticks to everything in the house except him." They both laughed and patted me in delight. So how could I even dream of hurting the man who, along with Nice Boy, would say such kind things about my fur?

Still, here was Joey, insisting to Xerxes that this was the man I'd all but massacred one time. She walked over to me now where I lay. "Dork," she shouted, climbing up on my face. I lifted my head off the floor again to show I was awake. Joey pulled my ear flap back and bawled into my ear: "Are you awake, Dork?" Sometimes I seriously wondered if Joey didn't go out of her way to be annoying. "Tell us about the time you nearly murdered the mailman."

"Oh, okay, if you insist," I said, pretending reluctance. In fact, I was secretly pleased, since my humans loved to talk about it all the time, making me the hero of the adventure.

The front doorbell rang that morning of the mishap, and I saw through the glass in the door that it was the mailman holding a package. That Man went out and answered it. I was resting from my labours on the hall floor, minding my own business, too tuckered out to even bother getting up. The evening before, I'd snuck away when I was out for my walk and stayed out the whole night on crucial matters. I was trying to meet up with the love of my life, a fabulously scented collie who lived down the street.

That night had turned out to be hectic. My sweetheart was locked up against her will in their house by her cruel human, and there were three other dogs besides me wooing her from her driveway. One was an irresponsible German police dog who should have been home guarding his own house; another was a hare-brained runaway cocker spaniel; and finally a Heinz-fifty-seven-varieties St. John's crackie.

There was tension in the air, especially between me and the police dog, involving a lot of impressive growling, strutting, and raised hackles. My worthy rival and I looked so good at it that the other two dogs were awestruck by us, and if they had any notion of right from wrong, they should have left the area. But, against all common sense, they stayed, and it was that silly crackie who caused all the trouble that night. He yapped and yelped without let-up, so that the adorable collie's cruel man came out of the house with a hockey stick to drive us away. Of course, that was ridiculous: my love was so strong that there was no way I was going to move away, and indeed I proved my devotion by getting whacked on the rear end with that hockey stick before I beat an honourable retreat.

Alas, all my efforts and sacrifice were to no avail that night, because I was not able to meet up with my true love. At daylight I could see her face at her window gazing out at me in adoration, but by now I was hungry. So I ran back home for my breakfast. Nice Boy let me in, wondered where I'd been all night, and gave me my meal. A little later that same morning, when That Man opened the front door to talk to the mailman, I suddenly woke up from my nap in the hall, smelling the delightful fragrance of love in the air from my darling collie, which proclaimed her undying ardour for me. And it was so strong that I knew she must be outside her house having a walk right now, so I—

Here Joey interrupted me. "Dorky, excuse me, but I have to clarify a point. This beloved lady collie of yours, the sweet doggykins you adored so much and were willing to risk life and limb for against all other dogs and humans alike . . . may I ask what her name was?"

"Her name? Er, ah . . . that's a secret, Joey. I don't kiss and tell."

"You mean you don't even know her name, and you never did. Do you hear that, Herpes? This is way more serious than I first thought. We've definitely got to fix him. Dork is a psychopathic, serial lover-boy, completely under the control of his raging hormones."

"Yes, it's a sad case," said Xerxes, shaking his head gloomily. "We've got to figure out how to save him from that, for sure."

"That wasn't true what you just said, Joey," I said. "That collie was the love of my life. I was passionately in love with her for more than two weeks."

"Let's give this Lab a lifetime achievement award," said Joey. "Okay, tell us what happened next with the mailman, Dork."

"My mind is a little unclear on the details of what happened next. I do recall rising off the floor to my paws and being propelled by the powerful force of my love toward that open door. Our family tradition maintains that I bolted right by That Man, pushing him aside as if he were a feather, and flew out the door like a cannonball. Regretfully, without my knowledge or blame—I certainly had nothing to do with him being in my way like that—I happened to collide with the mailman, who was standing there. And I think he might have fallen down a little bit."

"Might have fallen down a little bit?" scoffed Joey. "According to That Man, the mailman went butt over teakettle, tumbling across the lawn and into the rhododendrons. It is reliably reported he had to visit a physiotherapist for the next six months. And the post office threatened to stop delivering mail here altogether."

"Yeah, a gross overreaction to an unavoidable mishap," I said. "And it never happened again."

"No, because the mailman never rang the doorbell again. He always poked a notice in the mailbox after that, if there were any packages. Don't you remember That Man complaining about always having to go to the postal outlet to pick up packages because you, Dork, had all the mail deliverers too terrified to ring the doorbell?"

"Don't tell me you heard That Man complaining about me again," I said. "That comes as a big shock. Now, don't get me wrong. I love him dearly, but he does have unresolved issues, like not being able to accept gracefully being second-in-command."

"I hope you're right about that, Dork," said Joey, "because his frustrated ambition may make him take you to the vet and have the job done, just for his own satisfaction. I know that's what I'd do if I was him. And we haven't even mentioned yet the tragic case of poor Granny's foot, last year. Remember that, Herp?"

"Why, what happened to poor Granny's foot?" asked Xerxes.

"Herpes, I thought you lived here. Don't you remember how Granny was sitting peacefully in the kitchen talking with Nice Woman, when Dork took it into his head to rear up and show his affection to Granny's foot in the most theatrical way possible? Granny dropped her teacup on the floor and jumped up screeching, 'Okay, everybody listen. This is it. It's either that blankety Durf or me!'"

"Oh yeah," said Xerxes. "It's all coming back. I guess I had that traumatic memory blocked out."

"Granny was great that time," I said. "You could tell she had a real thing for me, the way she always lumped the two of us together like that—'it's that blankety Durf or me.' Cool."

"I guess that's why we never saw hide nor hair of her in this house again for a month," said Joey. "Her 'real thing' for you was so strong."

"The time I remember best," said Xerxes, "was when Durf put

his front paws up on the shoulders of Nice Woman's friend and showed his affection to her in the same way. That Man had to yank and drag him away from her."

"That was all her own doing," I said. "She shouldn't have worn that sweater if she didn't want me to appreciate the delightful fragrance from her two Yorkies that was all over it."

"Yes, you could tell it was all her own doing," said Xerxes, becoming as sarcastic as Joey these days. "She screamed so loud, I took off upstairs frightened to death and hid under Nice Girl's bed. I don't know what happened after."

"What happened after was this," said Joey. "That Man said, 'The mutt has got to go.'"

"Oh, he was always saying foolish old stuff like that," I said, "just trying to be top dog. He never meant any of it. Look how fast he backed off when Nice Boy and Nice Girl said they'd run away if Durf had to go."

"Oh, he meant it, Dorky. All you got was a reprieve because he loves the kids so much. But I'd say you're on very thin ice around here. One more act of idiocy and I can hear you now, 'Howdy cousin Old Yeller. It looks right homey up here in doggy heaven.'"

"Heaven? Gosh, that sounds serious, Joella."

"It certainly is, Herpes. So we've got to get him fixed and improved to keep that from happening."

"Goodness knows I'm all for improving Durf," said Xerxes. "But how are we going to do it?"

Joey grinned fiendishly. "Herpes, we'll find a way. We have to. Dork is our 'friend.'" She made scare quotes in the air with her paw. "It's just a matter of getting That Man in the right mood. I heard him say after the Granny incident that he'd love to get it done."

"He did not say that," I barked. "He said that, unfortunately, it's too late now. Durf is too old. That Man said clearly that he would not feel right having it done to an adult dog."

"Let's see if he feels a little more right about it next time you go postal or get too affectionate with someone," said Joey. "Dorky, if I were you, I'd take your reprieve as very temporary—purely on a day-to-day basis. Because if That Man doesn't have it done, Herpes and I will do it ourselves, some dark night."

"Sounds good," said Xerxes.

Joey certainly had a talent for spooking someone out. I slept with my back to the wall for a few nights.

Chapter 7

The Face That Gets Me Off with Murder Every Time, Nearly

Except for when they ganged up on me like that, Xerxes and Joey weren't chums. They didn't treat each other as equals or give the impression they even liked one another. The aristocratic cat considered the tabby to be a low-life ruffian and the barn cat considered the Persian to be an effete dimwit. On many days, for all three of us, a lot of our time was filled, not with camaraderie, but with naps. Joey and I managed to sneak out of the house every so often, to go our separate ways. But Xerxes never went outside in those days, and it was only later that he accepted Joey's challenge to venture out the door a couple of times, with results that would dismay everyone.

Meanwhile, one occasional activity which brought Joey and me together in the house happened in the late afternoons or in the evenings after supper. This was when That Man went up to his attic hideaway and tapped away in front of his computer screen. If the kids weren't around for me to play with, I would follow him up there out of a sense of duty, to supervise him and help him out. And it was a good thing I did, too, because he often asked my advice: "Now Durf, how do you suppose I'm going to get this character out of the mess he's in?"

I panted and wagged my tail to encourage him, and he would straightaway start playing his keyboard like a piano again. As I stood there looking at him, or lay on the floor next to him, dozing off, he didn't seem to mind that I had no idea what he was up to, until Joey told me, "He's writing his foolish old books."

Joey often came up to the attic with us, intruding on my mentoring time with That Man. I could see how she knew what That Man was doing. She hopped up on his desk and, to stop him from reading the pages he'd printed off and placed there, she lay on top of them. "He's always spying on us, Dork," she told me. "No way am I going to let him write a book about us."

That Man laughed at her lying there on his pages and tried to move her off, even lifting her from the desk and putting her down on the floor. But time after time she hopped up and plopped down on the pages again. I couldn't figure out why he didn't get mad at her.

He did get a break from it when Nice Girl arrived home. Xerxes never climbed up to the attic with us because, he said, "My limit is one flight of stairs. I'm not the daredevil type." So Xerxes was usually downstairs on the ground floor when Nice Girl came in the back door. From the top floor, Joey's ears swivelled till she picked up the sound of Nice Girl saying his name, "Hi Xerxes, how's my beautiful pussycat?" That was Joey's cue. She bolted down over both flights of stairs, sounding like a herd of elephants. In the kitchen, she ran right up to Xerxes and belted him across the cheek for daring to receive a greeting from Nice Girl. I could hear Nice Girl saying, "Joey, don't be mean to Xerks. I love you, too. Come here for your hug. Yes, there's a good kitty cat."

I knew enough not to go down to greet Nice Girl right away on those days. Even when she had tried to pay some attention to me before, my competing with the circling, purring, nuzzling cats caused me to hardly get a look-in.

After a few minutes of the sentimental stuff with Nice Girl, the person she carried on most schmaltzy with, Joey came scampering up over the stairs again and tore into the attic room. "That Herpes!" she said, flying by me to jump back up on That Man's pages. "Always cozying up to Nice Girl to get hugs and kisses behind my back."

When That Man became fed up with Joey hogging his papers, compared to me lying quietly on the floor providing mature companionship, he went over and rolled the window open with the handle. He did that even if it brought cold and gusty wind in, because it was the only way to entice Joey to jump down off his desk.

She leaped out the window onto the roof, where she galloped about the shingles, sounding again like a herd of stampeding elephants. I could never figure out how she managed to produce so loud a racket. It was extremely impressive. When I asked her, she said, "Come out on the roof, Dorky, and I'll teach you."

While Joey was on the roof sprinting around, chasing the pigeons—every day, the same routine—That Man would sit there grinning his head off at her. You'd think he'd get tired of the same old cat rigmarole day after day, but oh no! He never stopped being taken in by her put-on kittenish performance. She thought she was being funny when she invited me out on the roof, did she? Well, I'd show her.

One day I followed her toward the window. That Man looked up and said, "Lucky the window is too small, Durf, because if you went out there you'd slide off the roof and kill yourself." Imagine someone thinking that I, a dog, couldn't do anything a silly cat could do. He had a lot to learn. I jumped up on the ledge and pushed my head out. The window was the kind that opened from the side, and my plan was to crawl out through the gap. But I may have misjudged my size compared to the width of the opening. The kids always said I never really got used to growing up, and that was true, because I often thought I was smaller than I was when it came to squeezing through spaces. And today my shoulders wouldn't go through the opening of the window.

That Man shouted, "Durf, what on earth are you doing? Stop. Come back." He made me feel kind of foolish, as if I didn't have a clue what I was up to. I scrambled with all four paws to force myself out. The window burst off its lever and I fell forward. I found myself hanging from the windowsill by my hips, my hind paws and rear end inside, and all the rest of me outside. My head pointed down over the roof, which I now discovered was steeply sloped and only about five feet wide from the window. Below the roof—far, far below—was our concrete driveway. And that was where I was heading.

I was paralyzed with fear and couldn't move a muscle. Then I felt That Man's hands on my back, which encouraged me, and I started scrambling with all four legs. "For heaven's sake, stop," he roared. "You're going to pull yourself out on the roof and fall." He pushed down hard on my lower back to keep me from slipping out farther and bawled over his shoulder, "Help, Mrs. Rock, I'm up in the attic. I need help." Mrs. Rock was our new housekeeper. This was her first day here.

None too soon, I felt another pair of hands on my back, and That Man said, "Hold him down hard." He climbed up on the inside ledge and stretched out through the window, muttering, "Good Lord, I'm going to be killed." I felt his hand reaching my collar and making a few soft tugs. "I can't get any leverage without falling off the roof myself," he said. "Mrs. Rock, try to pull him back by the hips." When I started to help again, he got mad: "Durf, for the love of—*stop moving your legs.*"

Between the three of us, That Man and I finally managed to crawl back inside. I didn't even mind being half-strangled by his last couple of yanks on my collar. Joey now jumped in through the window and summed up my adventure: "Good first effort, Dork. We'll try it again in a year or two when That Man lets you back up in the attic again."

That Man spoiled Joey's idea, though: "I'm going to have bars put on that window," he said. "Good thing you were here, Mrs. Rock, or Durf and I would have both been killed."

I knew that Mrs. Rock liked me because, after she helped me complete my roof adventure that day, she might have shaken her head sometimes, but she grinned at me a lot.

The next day, I snuck outside when everyone was leaving for work and school. But soon I barked at the back door to come in because my paws were chilly from the icy rain and puddles everywhere. Mrs. Rock let me in and said, "Durf, you're all wet and muddy. Stay out there in the porch till you dry off." Then she pulled the kitchen door to and thought she'd closed it. Of course, it was only pup's play for me to push that warped, antique door open to get in the kitchen and sniff around the floor to see if any specks of food might have been dropped and missed.

Mrs. Rock had gone upstairs and I noticed that she'd left open the door to the laundry room off the kitchen. No one else had done that before, and I found now that the little room was balmy and comfortable. Inside I spotted a basket of freshly laundered towels. They were all warm and soft from the dryer and really smelled fresh. What better place for a cold, wet dog to have a comforting nap? I hopped on top of the towels and settled in for a dream about the true love of my life, the German boxer who lived across town. In my dream, the man who lived in the same house as my beloved boxer was shouting at me, "get out of here," and, "go away," as usual—no big deal—but I was a little disconcerted to hear him roar, "Durf!" How did he even know my name? The next roar of "Durf!" was accompanied by a poke in my ribs, not hard, but enough to wake me up to see Mrs. Rock standing over me with a broom in her hands, shouting my name.

I slid right off the towels, even though she didn't ask me to. It was as if I had a sixth-sense intuition out of the blue that I should get off. Then I realized that she wanted to have fun with the broom, so I stood there in a playful stance, looking at her, waiting for her next move.

"My heavens, what a mess!" she muttered. She must have been talking about Joey's food dish nearby, which had pieces of cat food scattered around it. Then she said, loud and clear, "DURF, ACT YOUR AGE." But I didn't quite get the point she was making at the time. Was I acting too old or too young? It made no difference because she put the towels back in the washer and dryer to warm them up again for my next time.

That afternoon, when Nice Boy and Nice Girl came home from school, Mrs. Rock bent over to look in the fridge, getting them "a healthy snack." I showed her my playful side again by rooting her from behind with my snout—the game Granny liked so much—and Mrs. Rock shouted it out again: "My glory! Durf, Act your age!" She put on a stern poker face herself, but the kids looked at each other and grinned, so I knew we were having fun.

One of the best bits of fun I had with Mrs. Rock happened the day I let the lobsters loose. That Man had a big box of live lobsters delivered to the house that he wanted to boil up for a dinner party that night. Mrs. Rock put the box on the kitchen table in a plastic bin for him and went upstairs with some clean laundry.

The oceany, fishy smell from the box insisted on being examined. I jumped up on a chair, climbed onto the table, and put my front paws on top of the box. Without warning, the plastic container, and the box in it, tipped over and tumbled off the table, down to the floor. The box lay on its side with the top now bulging open, and a lobster poked out its claws and antennae. By the time Mrs. Rock came down again, ten lobsters with rubber bands around their claws were crawling in every room. Xerxes was cowering under the kitchen table, Joey was stalking and pouncing on lobsters and batting them, and I was barking and yelping from one room to the other.

Just then That Man came in. He'd picked up the kids from school and come home early to start preparing his feast. I ran out to meet them, hearing Mrs. Rock in the hall shrieking, "Durf, act your age!" before she trotted into the kitchen with a lobster in each hand. "My glory, they're everywhere," she groaned.

The kids started shouting, "Durf, act your age!" and ran around with That Man, fetching lobsters and putting them back in the box. I pranced and jumped about and lowered myself on my front paws to join in the game. Mrs. Rock sighed loudly and threw her hands up in the air. What fun she and I had in those days.

Besides playing great games with me, Mrs. Rock also admired my acting skills. She had a favourite way of complimenting me on my dramatic ability. It started one day when she sat down to her lunch just as the phone rang. When she got up to answer it, I noticed that her back was turned, so naturally I took advantage of that, in my best Labrador retriever tradition, to stretch up to her plate on the table, delicately take her filet of cod in my teeth, and straightaway wolf it down in one gulp. By the time she hung up the phone and came back to the table, I was lying in the corner again "taking a nap."

"What happened to my codfish?" she blared. I opened my eyes, as if awakened, and raised my head to assume a look of concern. "Durf, did you steal my fish?" she demanded without a shred of evidence. I stood up and came over to her, something no guilty thief would ever do, turned my head on one side, cocked one floppy ear higher than the other, and looked at her with all the empathy I could muster in my melting brown eyes.

"Just look at him," she said. "He puts on that face that gets him off with murder every time." Throwing up her hands in her all-is-futile manner again, she went out to the dining room and sidled up to the liquor cabinet. She took out a bottle and hoisted it high enough to glug down a fair-sized slug of booze right out of the mouth of it. "I needs that, Durf," she said, patting me on the head, "after surviving you ever since I arrived here. You got me crucified."

Every day after that, whenever she needed to remark that my face was getting me away with murder, she went to the liquor cabinet and did it again—a different bottle every day. Then she patted me, smiled down at me, and gave me a hunk of cheese or meat. We were a good team.

The kids picked up on that saying of hers, too. If they weren't greeting me with, "Durf, act your age!" and laughing, they were waking me up from an innocent sleep with, "Durf, you've got that face on you that gets you off with murder every time." And they'd chuckle and hug me and play. Mrs. Rock's sayings brought a lot of fun and games into the house.

Naturally, I found it handy to have a face on me that got me off with murder. But I didn't find it so funny the day I was accused of murder for real. That happened just because I brought home some unusual bones which accidentally turned out to be human. I was lying down on the floor in the porch by the back door early in the morning, minding my own business, when the accusation of murder was made.

The front doorbell rang and I heard That Man coming down over the stairs to answer it. I didn't rush out, as I usually did, to greet whoever was there. I had an odour about me which, although it smelled pungently agreeable to me, could be the type of stink, my memory told me, that not all humans might appreciate. I heard That Man greeting the person at the door as Doctor something, who then said, "I was driving by your house on the way to the hospital and I thought I'd better let you know that there's a human scapula and a humerus on your front lawn."

That Man queried in a high voice, "A human what?" His tone perked my ears up. It sounded similar to whenever he was about to jump to an uncalled-for conclusion about me.

"A human shoulder blade and a human upper arm bone."

Call me psychic, but I sensed, from the way That Man now roared, "Durf!" that the depths of the dark closet off the porch, where the winter coats and boots were stored for the summer, would be a good place for me to skedaddle into and hang out for a while. Still, I had no idea what the fuss was all about. When I'd found those bones lying on the ground and brought them home, I did so because they were so interesting. I had never seen bones like them before and I figured my family would be fascinated, too. I was right about Nice Boy and Nice Girl, at least. They praised the bones later as "canine found art." That Man was not quite so impressed.

Before he could find me in the closet, Nice Boy came downstairs wondering why he was bellowing my name. I listened to father and son discussing the bones, with That Man speculating on whom I'd murdered in order to obtain them. I should have known that his fanatical ambition to rise from number two to number one around here would sooner or later drag me into a frame-up, with the way then cleared for him to take over after I was executed or jailed for life. But luckily, Nice Boy jumped in with some much-needed logic: when he and his dad went out the front door to size up the bones, he said, "They look really old."

Caught red-handed in his whopper, That Man had to acknowledge, "Okay, maybe, just maybe Durf didn't murder someone to get them." Then they chatted about the record-breaking torrential downpour of rain that had occurred a couple of days ago and caused washouts and flooding around St. John's. One flood took place in a well-known city cemetery and there were alarming reports on the news that at least one coffin and some bones floated to the surface.

"Of course, leave it to Durf to discover them," said That Man. "Okay, let's grab some old gloves we don't mind throwing away after. We'll put the bones in a garbage bag and I'll bring them back to the cemetery people."

The rest of the family was still sleeping, and while That Man and Nice Boy were outside gathering up my harvest of human bones, I left the closet to talk to the cats for a while about this silly, overblown bone situation. The highlight of our discussion was when Xerxes said, "It was a darn good thing you finally figured out you weren't human, Durf, or That Man would be accusing you of cannibalism, too, by now."

"You got that right, Xerks," I said. "But since he had to let me off with the murder rap, I wouldn't be surprised if he suddenly suppresses all the evidence that I'm a dog to frame me for cannibalism, yet."

Joey gazed at me for a long moment and then at Xerxes. She looked like she didn't know whether to laugh or cry. "You've raised some tough questions there, guys," she said at last. "When Dork chews on human bones, would he be a cannibal if the evidence that he is a dog is held back?"

"And what about if I didn't know they're human bones at all?" I asked. "That must get me off the hook for something."

Now Xerxes furrowed his brow and thought hard. "But can someone get off the hook for being a moron just because he's a nitwit?" he asked. "We must check that out, because I might be missing out on some big opportunities here, myself."

"Who would have thunk it?" sighed Joey. "In my own house, I'm surrounded by the world's top two philosophers. I mean, what are the odds?"

Just as we were about to plumb these questions properly to their depths, I heard the front door opening and That Man asking Nice Boy, "Where's Durf? I smelled that same stench in the house earlier. He must have brought it in with him."

"I haven't seen him. He was inside when I went to bed last night. Maybe someone let him out after?"

I took this as my cue to leap up from the floor and sneak back to the dark recesses of the closet and stay there—forever, if necessary.

Chapter 8

No Man is Indispensable, But a Dog Is

My time in the closet away from the family dragged on unbearably. I didn't know how much longer I could take this prolonged, torturous exile. At about the five-minute mark I heard That Man and Nice Boy and Nice Girl in the kitchen talking about making French toast for everyone's breakfast. "A little surprise for Mom when she comes down," said That Man.

What? Did he say surprise? More like shock wave. Nice Woman asked him once, "Where is it written in our marriage contract that the hubby is forbidden to be a little bit handy in the kitchen?" And he grinned so foolishly she could only smile and give him a pat on the shoulder. Talk about someone putting on a face that gets him off with murder all the time.

As That Man was taking the eggs out of the fridge now, he dropped three on the floor. I could hear the unmistakable splats of three raw eggs breaking as they landed. I tore out of the closet, heedless of possible anger misdirected at me for the appearance of the human bones, and nudged That Man, as he stared uselessly down, away from the disaster scene, and I took charge of the cleanup operation. In jig time I had licked up the three eggs, whites and yolks alike, leaving only the eggshells on the floor. I figured, after I'd just done all the heavy work, that even he had the wit to sweep a few eggshells into a dustpan. Meanwhile, he stood there gazing at me dumbfounded. "Did you see that?" he said to the kids. "Durf slurped up all the egg without getting one piece of shell in his mouth. That dog is a genius. He should train to be a brain surgeon."

At last, That Man was learning his place around here: I had the skills of a top dog and he didn't. Yet, what thanks did I get for my leadership beyond those empty words of praise? When Nice Woman came down now and asked what that smell was, he replied, "That would be the human remains on Durf." Tugging me by the collar out to the backyard, he told her about the bones found on the lawn, adding: "Durf will have to be left out back until he airs out enough for someone to give him a bath without gagging." There was gratitude for you—banished from the house in a *coup d'état* by That Man after rescuing him from his blundering folly with the eggs.

I soon forgave him again, though, because he redeemed himself when he later returned the human bones to the cemetery. He did not allege to the groundskeeper that I'd carried the bones away. He just said he'd found them on his lawn. That was a super-important favour he did for me there, because I couldn't risk being banned from that cemetery: the path through it was my shortcut from the house to that great little fish plant down in Quidi Vidi Village.

I learned an invaluable lesson when I saved That Man from his egg disaster: I was totally indispensable around here.

Which meant that no matter how mad he got at me over some misunderstanding of his, I knew it could not last, because soon after that my vital help would be needed again. Not only was I extremely helpful about the house every day of our lives, but often I was absolutely essential.

"No man is indispensable," I heard That Man say one time about himself, and he got that right. But I never heard him say that no dog is indispensable. How could he when the living proof to the contrary was constantly before his very eyes? He had but to tote up all the important jobs I did uncomplainingly every day: checking, whenever the doorbell rang, to see who was at the door before anyone else, and then wagging my tail as official greeter and nosing them with a friendly welcome if they came in; keeping tabs on Nice Girl's cats for her every minute of the day to make sure they weren't up to their usual mischief; waiting by the back door, if any family member was out, so that I could prance around in joy as soon as they came back. This was especially necessary if anyone came in the house with their hands and arms loaded with supermarket bags, because then we could all have fun chasing the apples and oranges and tins of tuna around the floor as they spilled out. And on and on it went . . . my list of helpful and essential services was already endless.

After my experience with the eggs, and the highly positive reaction from That Man, I knew that any time someone dropped messy food onto the floor, my humans would be depending on me to salvage the situation by performing my expert cleanup job. Sometimes, though, my family and Mrs. Rock got confused and sent me mixed signals. One time, a chicken casserole she was taking from the fridge slipped from her fingers and landed softly and upright on the floor. I experienced déjà vu from my experience as a pup with the chicken cacciatore back at the kennel, and I knew exactly what you had to do with a dropped container of chicken. I instantly sprang to my feet, ran over, and went to work. Oh, sure, Mrs. Rock tried to pick it up herself and cried, "Stop, Durf." But I came to the rescue by nosing the cover off and beginning to gobble up the contents.

I had a fair amount of the chicken cleaned up before she and Nice Boy pulled me off the mess, both of them shouting, "No, Durf, no!" I could not comprehend what they were doing. But when Mrs. Rock said, "Now I'm going to have to make the whole casserole again," I made a mental note to stand by and watch carefully when she did that, just in case there was another mess to be cleaned off the floor which she mightn't be able to handle without my help. My aid and support to everyone in this house went on twenty-four seven.

My responsibilities as boss of the cats were the most challenging of all my jobs. And talk about risky! Their lawless activities sometimes got me into trouble in spite of my complete innocence. Just listen to this tragedy: soon after that silly tempest in a teapot over the human bones, Nice Woman baked a cake and some cookies to celebrate That Man's birthday. He was in the other room watching television with the kids. She placed all the baked goodies on the kitchen table to cool. "No one is to go in the kitchen till I get back," she said, closing the door and heading for the bathroom. "I haven't had a chance to put the cake and cookies away."

"Okay, Herpes, we've got to move fast," said Joey from the hall. "We've only got about three minutes, max. Dork, listen up." She came over to me and banged me on the nose to make sure she had my attention. "You get over there and use your oversized hulk to shove the door open for us."

But the essence of intelligence is learning from one's experiences, and I had suspicions that I'd been down that road before when I helped Zippo the sausage dog to push Granny's kitchen door open that time. "No way, Joey," I said. "I've still got mixed feelings from everything that happened when I played Zippo's baked-ham game."

"Don't you be so foolish, Dork. The whole family has been talking about that magnificent ham caper and laughing their heads off ever since. They loved it. Come on."

"I don't know, Joey. Don't you think That Man has been acting rather cold toward me, from when he accused me of everything under the sun over those human bones?"

"Cold? No. I heard him say he never saw anything so cute."

Xerxes jumped in. "I never heard him say it was cute, Joella. I only heard him say it was disgusting."

"Cute? Disgusting? It's easy for a cat of restricted brainpower to confuse those two words, Herpes. So button up, okay? We're losing time here. Let's go, Dork. Do it. As a favour to your best friends."

While I stood there pondering the uncomfortable outcome every time I did something as a favour for a "best friend," Joey said, "Oh, thanks a lot, Dork. Just goes to show you can never depend on a grave robber for a favour." She ran back from the door a few feet and said, "Look out. Gangway." Then she galloped toward the door and pounced at it, twisting in mid-air and striking the door with all four paws, especially her hind ones. It was very impressive. She had drop-kicked the door open a couple of inches. "Come on, Herpes. We're running out of time. No, not you, Dork. I don't want human remains on my cookies, thank you very much. And while we're on the subject, no more kissing on the lips in the future, okay?"

"Are you sure this is going to be all right with Nice Woman, Joella?" asked Xerxes as the cats squeezed the door open wide enough to get through.

"Of course it'll be all right, Herpes. Nice Woman gave me the go-ahead, to get me to live here, to do this any time I feel like it. Come on, we don't have time to gab about this before she comes back out." They hopped up on chairs.

"How come I've never heard about you doing it before, then?" Xerxes followed Joey in jumping onto the table.

"That just proves my point, Herpes. If I wasn't allowed to do this, you certainly would have heard about it. I rest my case."

"That makes sense," said Xerxes.

"All right, Herp," said Joey, crouching down by the cake covered with chocolate icing. "Let's kick butt." She started right in with long licks right across the glazed top. Xerxes chose a cupcake with vanilla icing and went to work.

Within a minute they had tongued the top of every frosted cake and cookie on the table. Then Joey heard the bathroom door opening and said, "Gotta vamoose, Herpes. Come on, let's go." She bounded off the table and scooted out the door.

Xerxes followed, protesting, "But Joella, it's only Nice Woman coming back." Joey seemed so intent on disappearing that Xerxes just kept following her out the door. By the time Nice Woman walked back to the kitchen, she only saw the fluffy blue tail vanishing around a corner.

"Durf," she called out to me. "How did this door get open?" Then she went in and examined her baked goods on the table.

"Every single one ruined," she said. "Did you push it open and let the cats in?" She started picking up cookies and cake and dumping them in the garbage pail. "I'm very disappointed in you, Durf." I put on every getting-away-with-murder face I could think of and went over and lay my head against her to show how innocent I was, but all to no avail. She pushed me away and ignored me, except to look at me with a sad, upset face.

All that disapproval and unhappiness coming at me from Nice Woman was heartbreaking. I wouldn't have minded it if That Man was doing it; I was used to that. I looked down the hall. Joey and Xerxes were now back in plain sight. A morsel of vanilla icing was weighing down one of Xerxes's whiskers and Joey was sitting there licking her paw with a tongue still brown with chocolate.

Then Joey came over to me and said, "See, Dork? You should have pushed the door open for us, like I asked. Then you could've had a cupcake or two at least, but now here you are with nothing and still getting all the blame."

"Yeah, I know, Joey. I was really stupid not to give you a hand."

"And I didn't need you, anyway. I was only trying to make you feel a bit useful around here and let you share in the booty, because as you plainly saw, I was quite capable of opening the door myself."

"That was amazing, Joella," said Xerxes. "Where did you learn to do that?"

"My mother taught me out at the barn. She told me she learned it from watching the Wide World of Wrestling with the caretaker on his TV out there. I saw her use it on a big dog that came around one time frightening the horses. Sent him packing with his tail between his legs, yelping his head off. I can teach you to do it if you want, Herpes."

"Er, I might take a pass on that, Joella. I'm not sure my elite breeding makes it acceptable for me to employ any wrestling techniques at all, let alone those taught by a female cat who learned them in a barn." He laid his ears back and closed his eyes to ready himself for a clout, in case he'd just said something Joey mightn't appreciate. He never seemed to know for sure, but this time he was right. Joey moved toward him.

Before she could reach him, though, That Man approached and stood over us. "Everyone in the kitchen," he said. "Durf, Xerxes, Joey, I've got something for you all in there." We followed him in, naturally thinking there was at least a treat in it for us. The cats were too slow-witted to know the difference, but I should have known better. He was using that gruff sound and that stern face he always wore whenever he was about to act like he was the big boss around here.

The family was sitting around the kitchen table. "We're going to establish some rules of behaviour in this house," said That Man. "This free-for-all anarchy around here has gone on long enough." He picked up Xerxes, held him over the table, and said, "No, Xerxes. No table." Xerxes looked at me and at Joey, baffled. The fact that That Man repeated it about ten times did not improve Xerxes's grasp on whatever point he was seeking to make. Then he put Xerxes back on the floor and picked up Joey and repeated over and over the same words: "No, Joey. No table." Joey didn't look perplexed at all. She stretched herself out on That Man's hands and closed her eyes in contentment.

The problem he was having with impressing his message on Joey was that whenever he'd picked her up before, Joey had come to expect her favourite pastime. This consisted of lying on her side on his two hands and pretending she was an accordion. That

Man would gently stretch her out and compress her several times, parting his hands and bringing them together, back and forth, like a squeezebox, as she blissfully lay there, limp. If anything could cause Joey to burst into purring that sounded like an outboard motor, that was it. She lay herself out like that now, even though playing the accordion seemed to be far from That Man's intention. He tried to resist and kept yakking, and she kept lying in accordion position in his hands. Finally, he stifled a laugh and compressed and stretched her twice, then put her down on the floor.

Now it seemed to be my turn to play this new nonsensical game of his, whatever it was. He kept closing the kitchen door and pushing it open as he repeated the word "no" to me. What wasn't it that he did not want me to not do? Did he not want me to not close the door or to not open it? To help the poor fellow, I took a stab at it and went over, after he'd closed the door, and nosed it open to show that I got his message that he wanted me to do something or other with the door. "No, Durf," he said, "bad dog." What? Go figure. I wished That Man would make up his all-over-the-map mind and show better leadership skills if he truly aspired to inherit the top dogship from me when I retired and passed the torch.

When That Man's charade in the kitchen was over, Xerxes, Joey, and I went out to the living room for a summit meeting. Xerxes said, "What in heaven's name was that all about?"

"Darned if I know," I said.

"Beats me, too," said Joey, "but That Man did seem to be peeved about something. Usually he stretches me out and squeezes me together for as long as I want, but today he only did it twice and put me down. And me there in his hands purring my head off!"

"And he didn't stretch and squeeze me at all, which was

weird," said Xerxes. He had a sudden flash: "Hands up who thinks that That Man has no idea what he's supposed to be doing half the time." We all raised a paw.

"And did you hear him right out of the blue at the end?" I asked. "'No special treats until further notice.' I'm telling you guys, this could be serious. We've got to do something about it. But what?"

None of us had any idea what to do, mainly because we had no idea what it was we were supposed to be doing something about. Then, at supper, I had one of my brilliant flashes of insight that made me so indispensable.

Chapter 9

Joey Gives That Man a Perfect Pet

The idea came to me while the family was singing happy birthday to That Man. I noticed that Nice Woman and the kids brought to the table as they sang, not the usual big birthday cake with many candles on it, but a little cupcake with one lit candle sticking up from it. Putting it on the table in front of him, Nice Woman wished him happy birthday and said, "Luckily it's the thought that counts, because this is the best we could do in the circumstances. Your real cake is in the garbage pail, if you'd like to admire it."

Her husband said thank you and kissed her cheek and glanced over at me and the cats with a scowl. The kids looked at each other and then over at us, struggling, not entirely successfully, to keep down their cackles. At first I was thinking That Man was irritated because of the cake, but that couldn't be it. The kids seemed delighted with what had happened, even though they were the ones who loved cake more than anybody. Then I saw his family giving him their birthday presents, and bingo, I had it!

"Joey, I know why he's mad with you. You didn't give him a birthday present."

"What are you talking about, Dork? I never give him a present and he always loves me anyway. Besides, he was mad at me before he even knew I wasn't going to give him a present."

"Joey, will you stop putting roadblocks in the way of my attempts to help you out here? Do you want to get back in his good books again or not?"

"I wouldn't mind, but I'm not going to kill myself at it. And how would you know how to go about doing that, anyway? Sure, That Man is always on the outs with you."

"Yeah, but I'm a dog. And he's always trying to be top dog. It's a family rivalry thing going on with us. It's different with a cat. Cats don't have the head for that top-level management stuff, so they're no threat." Joey sat looking at me as if she was trying to decide whether she could be bothered coming over and clobbering me across the snout. I figured I'd better start fibbing up a storm: "That's because cats are more cultured, more refined, and just better all-round than dogs."

Joey sighed. "At last, you're finally making a pick of sense. So what would you do if you were me, Dork?"

"I'd give him a lovely gift."

"Like what? A lovely human skull from the graveyard to go with your lovely human bones?"

"No, not a beautiful dog gift, Joey. You need to give him a lovely cat gift. What's your favourite thing in the whole world?"

"That's easy. A pigeon, especially one still flapping its wings. Or maybe a rat I've cornered. It's a toss-up."

"Those would be good, Joey. But it might be a bit hard to get them into the house without attracting attention before you have a chance to surprise him with them. What else? Probably something smaller."

"What about a mouse? A mouse held between my teeth, still wriggling."

"Perfect," I said. "I bet he'd love that as a gift. I've heard Nice Boy and Nice Girl talking about the guinea pig, the hamster, and the gerbils they had here before I took over. So why wouldn't everyone, including That Man, like getting a live mouse as a pet?"

"Well, a mouse scooting around the house is a beautiful thing," said Joey. "You're right, Dorky. What's not to love? A mouse it is, then."

As soon as she said it, I started to have my doubts, not about whether a live mouse would be a good gift to someone normal, but whether That Man would really appreciate getting anything at all as a gift. Case in point: those interesting bones the other day. Oh sure, hindsight is twenty-twenty, but who could have known beforehand that they'd end up being a complete flop just because someone labelled them human? Then there was the time I dragged home that slab of beef I'd saved seconds before it was about to go in the garbage bin behind the supermarket. It had a beautiful strong smell, but oh no, old pucker-face couldn't get rid of it fast enough. Same story with that full bag of garbage I'd dragged home at considerable effort with the fragrance of decaying fish that made it such a prize possession. He was certainly able to control his raptures over that gift, too. But the peak of his ingratitude was over the whale blubber.

On that memorable day, I'd caught a fragrance wafting on the breeze of something unfamiliar but gloriously pungent. It led me, after hours of following my nose at a steady run, right down to the sea. There, on the beach in a remote cove, rested a huge dead whale. The body was covered with gulls and crows, and already a couple of dogs were on the massive hulk getting the jump on the rest of us. Judging by the thorough job they'd all done of stripping away pieces of skin and releasing the delightful aroma of the blubber below, the whale had been there, seasoning magnificently, for a few days. I couldn't resist frolicking about on the bloated corpse myself for a while before I tore off a big piece of blubber to bring home to my family.

It was dark when I finally got back to the house, exhausted from half-dragging and half-carrying the morsel of blubber, and scratched at our door. Even before the door opened, I heard That Man saying, "Good Lord, what's that stink?" So far, so good. But when he turned on the outside light and opened the door and saw me, he bawled, "What is that you're covered with? No, don't come in here. You're filthy and you smell to high heaven. What's that in your mouth? No, don't bring that in the house. Drop it, DROP it! Oh my God, the stench! You're going out in the backyard for the night." Drama queen or what?

The next morning, he and Nice Boy came out to the backyard with rubber gloves on. That Man was carrying a shovel. He told Nice Boy that they'd have to give the shovel a good hosing down, too, since he'd used it last night to lift the hunk of blubber into a double garbage bag for the dump. For the dump? "Oh, you're welcome," I woofed. Did I sound sarcastic over his reaction to my gift? Well, I'm sorry, but I meant every word of it. And what was that he'd just said: give the shovel a good hosing down, *too*? What did he mean by that scary "too," exactly? I should have realized from the grim look on Nice Boy's usual sunny face that his dad was up to no good again.

Suddenly, they were spraying vile-tasting soap all over me, and turning a blast of water from the hose on me, which could have been fun, but then they held me in place and went seriously to work on me with a scrubbing brush. In spite of that, according to them, their efforts were in vain. A lot of "it" just wouldn't come off. Then, with barely enough time for me to grab a quick breakfast from my bowl, which they had without explanation brought out to the backyard, they led me on a leash to the car. There they covered the back seat and floor with towels, loaded me on board, and took me to this torture chamber.

It's too traumatic to recall all the details of the cruel and unusual punishment the torturers inflicted on me there. Suffice it to say that, after yet more hosing and scrubbing, plus blow-drying, I came home looking and feeling like a stuffed toy animal made of polyester plush. In places, my fur was sticking straight up. Well, what could you expect when they spent the day rubbing my fur the wrong way? Nice Boy said, when he put his hands on me, that I felt just like one of those big fuzzy teddy bears you'd win down at the regatta, and he hugged me. I know he was too kind to deliberately embarrass me, but I was mortified.

I walked around the house paying no attention to the cats saying how much they admired my "new look" and sniggering. And I tried to be brave when the humans babied me and cooed at me as if they were Granny with Zippo the sausage. I didn't go outside the house or the backyard for a week for fear of being seen in this state on the streets by some of my twisty-tailed brigade, who, before my visit to the pet grooming torture chamber, had looked up to me as their guru and godfather.

Those were the gruesome flashbacks about my blubber gift that I suffered right after I'd encouraged Joey to give That

Man a live mouse as a gift. They created serious misgivings in my mind over the whole idea of any kind of a gift to him. But then I thought, even if That Man, because of the peculiar way he was, didn't appreciate her gift any more than he appreciated mine, well, no real harm would be done. In fact, it could well be a positive benefit for Joey. It would be a maturing experience for her to be on the receiving end of utter rejection. Because I knew that such toughening experiences had made a mature adult dog out of me.

Now, it would have been fairly easy to find a mouse outside the house, but Joey was a thinker. She figured that it might be counterproductive to bring a mouse into the house in her jaws. Whoever let her in would see the mouse and might start screeching that he or she wanted it, and that could cause a rift in the family. Hence, the mouse would have to come from inside the house and be caught when no one was looking. That conclusion kept Joey on the prowl from room to room for five or six nights in a row before she found one.

Early one morning, around daybreak, she called, "Dork, Herpes, come in here. Look. Jackpot." When we ran into the kitchen, Joey was in a corner, toying with her gift-mouse with one paw.

"Joella," said Xerxes, "you are a genius. But are we sure about this particular mouse? Do we think That Man will want a pet mouse who's stupid enough to come into a house that has two cats?"

Joey said, "I don't remember promising to give him a rocket-scientist rodent. Come on over, Herp, and have a bit of fun with it."

Xerxes shrunk back. "Er, I'm not really the sportsy type. Maybe Durf would like to."

"I would if it was a mallard duck or a Canada goose, but a mouse is more of a cat thing. And I don't want to spoil your moment, Joey."

"Thanks, Dork. This is going to be great. Well, here goes nothin.'" She was just oozing false modesty and making me jealous over the popularity she was going to have with That Man. She took the mouse between her jaws, carefully making sure that its wiggling legs were hanging down, and trotted proudly out of the kitchen toward the stairs, heading up to That Man asleep in his bed.

"Break a leg, Joella," Xerxes called after her.

"Come on, let's go up," I said to him. "We just gotta see the delighted look on his face."

We followed quietly behind and entered the bedroom barely in time to see Joey jump up on the bed where Nice Woman and That Man lay blissfully sleeping. Conveniently for Joey, he was lying on his back. I've never seen a cat so lucky. Joey crept up to his head, moving very carefully, to make the joy of the surprise gift all the greater. She straddled his neck, holding the mouse over his face. Then she meowed, hard to do with a mouse in your mouth, but the garbled sound that came out was enough to wake up That Man. Even in the dim light I could see his eyes jerk wide open, gleaming and flashing like the eyes of a rabbit in night traffic as they strained to focus on the unidentified, but clearly gruesome, object.

To hear him tell it afterwards, he didn't know at that moment if he was actually awake or, as he hoped, just having a new worst nightmare of dangling rodent legs, wriggling and writhing, two inches above his face. Joey, sensing That Man's confusion about how he should accept the gift, used her superb feline intuition to resolve all his doubts by dropping the squeaking, squirming mouse from her mouth right onto his mouth. A professional relay team could not have effected a more perfect transfer.

Now, immature humans like That Man have a tendency to overreact to surprising events, however charming. So it's difficult for me as a dog to convey with one hundred per cent accuracy what he did next. I know I capture only a little of the sound that came out of his mouth when I say that he went, "AWWWRRRRRGGGHHHH!!!" followed by several short, pithy sounds that his own children were not allowed to say, but which he must have learned from Granny. Similarly, don't ask me to explain how he went from the position of lying flat on his back in bed to instantly standing upright on his feet on that bed, with no observable transition between the horizontal and vertical positions. Perhaps quantum physics has the answer.

Meanwhile, the abrupt upward movement of That Man, plus the thrust of his hands, sent Joey flying through the air across the room. It was a testament to her aerial skills that she managed to land on all fours on the opposite wall before sliding down to the floor.

Nice Woman had awakened to That Man's screech as he bounced on their bed, trying to remove with hysterical hand motions something invisible, but apparently horrendous, from his face. She gaped at Joey slipping down the wall for no reason and sauntering toward me and Xerxes as we sat quietly there, rendered inert by the turn of events.

Nice Woman now very likely joined us in following with our eyes the demented mouse, not currently squeaking, but shrieking, as it hurtled around the room before escaping out the door to heaven knows where, although Xerxes did hazard a serious guess:

"It might be safe to assume that it won't be resuming its career as a house mouse any time soon."

"Oh, very astute, Herpes," growled Joey as the three of us courteously vacated the upstairs so that husband and wife could have the privacy of their bedroom. "And you, Dork—any theories on why that didn't seem to go as well as you suggested it would?"

"Absolutely none, Joey. Beforehand, it looked to me like it was going to be a good operation." In the kitchen, Joey searched my face for any telltale smirks, and it was pure luck she didn't see any because, in fact, what had happened, though opposite to what I'd intended, had gone better than my wildest dreams. Oh, I loved Joey dearly, but she could be a sarcastic smart aleck sometimes, and it was a great pleasure, as her friend and protector, to witness her complete downfall.

Xerxes must have agreed because he said, "It wasn't all bad, Joella. It's good for someone as smart as you to be put in your place sometimes. Keeps you from getting a swelled head."

"A swelled head? I've never seen one of those," said Joey. "Let's see what a swelled head looks like." She advanced on Xerxes menacingly.

Luckily for Xerxes, Mrs. Rock, the nice housekeeper, arrived, and nearly got me killed. "Good morning, Durf," she said. "What have you been up to already, this early? You've got that face on you that gets you off with murder every time."

Joey stopped and gazed back at me hard, paw raised and claws out. I said, "This pleasant, innocent look is not my fault. It's a defect in the architecture of my face."

"Yeah, well, the time has come for me to redesign the architecture."

But suddenly we heard a squawk from on high: "My God, there's mouse droppings in the bed."

Mrs. Rock rushed out of the kitchen and up the stairs. Before long she trooped back down with Nice Woman and That Man, all carrying at the length of their arms the sheets, the duvet cover, the pillow slips, and the bedspread. They paraded through the kitchen out to the backyard, where they gave all the bedclothes a good shake, and then back inside to cram it into the washer in the laundry room. As they passed us both times, the three of us sat there looking up at them with eyes that said, "Be sure to let us know if we can help." That Man gave each of us, but especially Joey, a glower that could easily be construed as antisocial, if not homicidal.

Joey must have sensed That Man's mood, too, because she said, "Guys, I think we better bounce." We slowly tiptoed toward the door, intending to disperse ourselves into the nether regions of the house for the normal cooling-off period. But That Man was too quick for us. He lunged for the door and shut it, trapping us with him alone in the kitchen. There was nothing for the three of us to do now but swarm him with love. While I nudged his hand with my snout and assumed my "let's play" stance, the cats each circled a leg, tails held high, nuzzling his shins with nose and ears and purring to beat the band.

That Man hissed between a whisper and a shriek, "Don't touch me, don't touch me, don't touch me!" and warded us off with ungentle flailing of all four limbs. Then he sat down on a chair and started in: "Now, you animals listen to me very carefully. Because this is a matter of life and death for you. I'm going to tell you about the tragic breakdown in relations between our family cat and my martyred mother, when I was a boy."

He and his young brothers, he said, had a cat eerily similar to Joey, except that he was a male. They named him Sweetface. Which, his mom declared, was like giving the name Bambi to Attila the Hun. The kids loved Sweetface for his amusing adventures, but their mother's early reservations about him only increased as time went on. She could always tell, just by the look of him, that whatever was coming from his direction was not going to be delightful.

There was no denying Sweetface's intelligence. He taught himself to turn on the tap in the bathtub, which was deemed cute until he did it one weekend when everyone was out and the plug, mysteriously, happened to be in the drain. The tub overflowed and flooded the house. Then, he learned how to open a basement window by turning the handle, which allowed him to get out when he was down there, but which also allowed a couple of amorous female cats with fleas to have the run of the house with him for most of the day while no one was home. The house, and Sweetface, had to be professionally fumigated.

One question That Man's mother asked frequently was, "If that cat is as smart as you kids claim he is, why doesn't he use his Kitty Litter every time instead of the living room carpet twice a week?" Then came the night she turned back the covers on her matrimonial bed before going to the bathroom. When she returned, tired and dying to get in bed, she glimpsed Sweetface's tail withdrawing from the room, and then she noticed a giant, slimy hairball in the centre of a widening wet stain on her fresh percale sheets. Her husband found her sitting on the floor beside the bed, quietly weeping.

That Man stopped in his narration. He looked hard at Xerxes, Joey, and me before stating, "Now this is the part I want you to listen to closely, as if your lives depend on it. Because they do." We three looked at each other. Why did he think he needed to say that? Sweetface's fun with his family was so outstanding that we were already all ears. If we'd had fingers we would have been taking notes for our own use.

Right outside their house, said That Man, was a bus stop. He noticed that, over the next few days, his mother gazed out the window whenever she heard the motor or brakes of the bus outside, and she smiled pitilessly. An unusual amount of whispering was also taking place between his mother and father.

Normally their father was long gone to work before the kids left for school. But one morning soon after, he was still in the kitchen sipping his coffee when they departed.

That afternoon, each child arriving home from school had the same question: "Where's Sweetface?" And each child received the same answer from Mom: "Sweetface got on the bus, my darling. I happened to be looking out the window when a Mainline Bus stopped, and I saw Sweetface getting on. The bus left before I could go out and rescue him, and when I called the bus company, they said he must have jumped off again along the way because there was no sign of him on board. We can only hope he'll find his way back home." Her anxious hope about Sweetface's return did not seem to match the serene look in her eyes.

When their dad got home for supper, he said that he knew, sadly, about Sweetface; their mom had been so distraught about it that she'd called him at work. Everyone was miserable about the cat's disappearance for a while, but when the kids started saying they had to get another cat, the answer was always, "We've got to give Sweetface a fair chance to make it home first, and if, God forbid, he's gone to pussy heaven, we must have a decent period of grief for him. A couple of years wouldn't be too long to mourn such a superb cat." Protest and beg all they wanted, their mother would not relent in her devotion to remembering Sweetface.

It was only when he looked back on those days later, That Man told us three now, that he fully realized that, after Sweetface, quote-unquote, "got on the bus," all the whispering between his mother and father abruptly stopped, and from then on it was replaced with a contented sigh, and you could only call it a knowing smile every time they caught each other's eye.

Now in the kitchen, That Man studied me and Joey and Xerxes, one after the other, silently, soberly, for long enough to make us squirm in suspense. What morsel of delight could be coming next in his tale? Then he stood up from his chair. "The moral to the story is this," he said, smiling down at us, looking like a cross between Mother Theresa and Count Dracula. "It's possible for a pet, however lovable he or she may be, to end up getting on the bus . . . the heartbreak bus of no return. Because, my three sweet-faces, there's always a bus arriving and departing."

That Man marched out of the kitchen and upstairs with conviction, and we three moseyed out to the hall. Xerxes said, "That was a great story. Do you think he was serious about getting us a ride on the bus? That'd be outstanding."

"I'm sure he was," I said. "He sounded very sincere about it."

"Maybe a touch too sincere," said Joey, gravely. She was always hard to enthuse.

"Sweetface sounded like a pretty good cat," said Xerxes. "I wish I could be like that, all carefree and heroic, but I'm way too trustworthy and dependable, almost to the point of being a bit square. Now, don't let this go to your head, Joella, but Sweetface seemed to be a lot like you. Except he was a tomcat, of course, and you're only a girl cat."

Joey remained strangely still, moving only enough to bat Xerxes half-heartedly on the chin while saying, "Yeah, Herp, it would be really grand to be a tomcat like you." Then, after a while, she asked thoughtfully, "Dork, do you think That Man is a member of the Mafia?"

"He could be, Joey. He's got everything else wrong with him. He's obsessive-compulsive over keeping the house stink-free, and a real anal-retentive takeover nut, and he has an overdeveloped top-dog complex, and a sociopathic lack of empathy when it comes to gift-giving. So why wouldn't he be in the Mafia, too?"

"Durf, my goodness, where did you learn all those hard words about That Man?" asked Xerxes.

"Watching the soaps on TV every afternoon with Mrs. Rock. Those shows are really educational."

Joey said, "That's where I got the idea he was in the Mafia, too, from television. I watched a gangster show with him one night. And then, a few minutes ago, when he was talking about us getting on the bus, it was almost like he was making a thinly veiled threat, exactly like the Mafia guy did in the show. And he kept looking right at me with the hairy eyeball, like the gangster did to people before they mysteriously disappeared, never to be seen again. Oh, call me paranoid by all means, but I'm thinking maybe I'd better watch my step for a little while until I figure out what's up with him."

"No, Joey, don't start thinking like that," I said. "You just have to keep on figuring out ways to bond better with him."

"You're probably right, Dorky, I appreciate the advice. Too bad that mouse got away. That must've been what made him mad.

The next time a mouse comes in the house, I'll try again. Maybe this time I'll wait till he's watching TV and jump up and drop it right on his head from behind, as a better surprise. Something like that."

"Now that's good thinking, Joey. Play our cards right and we'll have that bus ride yet."

"Yayyy," said Xerxes. "I'm counting on you guys to pull it off."

Chapter 10

My Unholy Alliance with the Cats Backfires

Our family didn't want Xerxes to go outside the house. He'd get disoriented, they said. And usually he showed no desire himself to venture outside. Even if someone accidentally left the back door open, he hardly went near it. But Joey was always pestering him to go outside with her, not for the company, she said, but on principle: she couldn't believe that there was really a cat in existence who didn't want to go outside and hunt. Spotting the door ajar one day, she urged, "Come on, Herpes, now's your chance. Run out behind me."

Xerxes replied, "I'd love to, Joella, but I'm not really the outdoorsy type, because Nice Girl is afraid I'm so beautiful that someone might kidnap me, and I just know she's right. So, I'm happy just being a house cat."

Impatiently, Joey heard out Xerxes's whinging explanation, and decided to try to shame him into going out: "House cat? Is that the same as scaredy-cat, Herpes?"

But Xerxes replied proudly, "Yes, Joella, I believe it is."

Joey sighed at her failed ploy. "What hope is there for the world?" she groaned. But she only grew more determined to change Xerxes into a real tomcat. "Do it just this once, Herp. Then it will be over and done with and you'll never have to do it again. You can't go to the pussy heaven That Man promised us, when we licked the cupcakes, without ever going outside once before you die. I'll be with you out there as your bodyguard. I'll get Dorky to protect you, too. And if, after all that security, someone still wants to kidnap that snub nose, and those bulging yellow eyeballs, and that flat face, don't worry, I'll pay the ransom myself."

I knew that Xerxes sometimes did look at an open door with mixed feelings. Yes, he wanted to remain the family's pure house cat, but deep down, secretly, he harboured the remains of an instinct to be a wild, adventurous, devil-may-care tomcat. So I was only a little surprised to hear him say to Joey one day, "Oh, okay, I suppose. Just for half a minute."

I was lying on the floor, dozing and listening to their boring cat talk. I knew the door was open, but there were no fragrances coming in from the love of my life, the whippet up the road, and it wasn't garbage day, so there was nothing important to be achieved outside, and I just lay there topping up my night's sleep. But Joey yelled, "Dork, snap out of it. The door is open. What on earth are you waiting for?" When I merely raised my head indifferently, she said, "Are you out of your mind? This is Tuesday at the supermarket."

I had no idea what Tuesday at the supermarket might mean, but it sounded essential to life itself. I hopped up and ran out the door, thinking that, when it came to cats, sometimes Joey wasn't such a bad one. Outside, That Man was lifting something heavy out of the trunk of his car to bring into the house. When I ran by, diverting his attention from Joey and Xerxes on the other side, he stood up straight and shouted, "Durf, come back. Here, Durf!"

Ever since the uptight neighbour across the street had rung our doorbell and stood there with a hammer in one hand, rhythmically hitting the palm of the other with it and carping insanely on about how a certain dog's days were numbered if he didn't stop rooting the bags out of his garbage can, That Man started insisting that I had to be on a leash whenever I went out. Therefore, I couldn't, in common sense, respond to his call to me now as I ran down the sidewalk in the direction of the supermarket, sniffing the breeze. I heard That Man say later that he hadn't noticed Joey and Xerxes creeping out before he carried his big package into the house and closed the door. I had to remember that favour I did those cats, for the next time they told me to stop being an idiot, trying to boss them around.

When Nice Girl got home, she noticed the absence of both cats right away and raised the alarm. I was already back, nursing the place on my hide where a man outside the supermarket had inexplicably raised his boot behind him in the air and unleashed it unerringly at my backside. What an immature psychopath. And greedy! Keeping that whole truckload of meat, every shred of it, for himself.

Nice Boy put a leash on my neck, and he and Nice Girl and I ran outside to find Xerxes. We went about five steps before we found him. He was on the lawn next door, crouching behind a shrub a few feet from our driveway. When he saw us coming, he said to me, "Oh, thank heavens, a search party. Because I'm well and truly lost. I think I was wandering about in circles just like I saw them do in the Gobi Desert on TV."

Nice Girl picked him up and cradled him in her arms, cooing lovingly, "Silly boy. What were you thinking, to come out here?"

"Xerks," I said over his purrs, "see that car there in our driveway?"

"The what? Oh yeah. So that's a car."

"Yes, it's That Man's car. And Nice Woman has one, too. But it's not here right now."

"Good," said Xerxes. "Because two cars would be complicated."

"And see that big green wall on the other side of the car?"

"The wall, the wall, the big green wall—where did you say it is again?"

"Right there in front of us, about ten feet away, with the door in it."

"Oh yes, now I see it. What about it?"

"That's our house."

"Our house? You mean where we live? Well, I'll be. You learn something new every day."

"What happened to Joey, by the way?" I asked him.

"She spotted a squirrel in a tree, way down the road, and took off like a scalded cat. I don't know why. You'd swear by the look of her that she was one of those lionesses you see on TV with a litter to feed."

That night, at supper, with Joey home, too, Nice Girl said that everybody had to be more careful not to leave any doors open, because "when Xerxes gets out, he becomes a little bit confused."

"I think she got that right, Xerxes," I said.

"She sure did," Xerxes said, gazing proudly at her. "She's a very smart young lady."

"I agree she's really smart," said Joey, "which makes it all the more surprising that she only said you were confused, and left out 'befuddled and baffled and bewildered.'" Although Joey had been back home for an hour, she was still out of sorts with Xerxes because, if he'd helped, the squirrel might not have evaded her earlier.

"Good point," said Xerxes. "Maybe she's saving those extra words for the next time my sister cat talks me into a foolhardy excursion outside, only to abandon me at the moment of greatest peril."

Joey sighed and got up. "Herpes, you're lucky Nice Girl is looking right at us or I'd come over there." She walked out, shaking her head. When she'd asked Xerxes why he hadn't joined her in stalking the squirrel as any normal cat would have done, he replied, "Whaaat? Chase a squirrel up a tree and have him drop nuts on my head? Joella, are you demented?"

Being polar opposites, Xerxes and Joey were not famous for their teamwork. Joey had limited patience with Xerxes's aristocratic pride in his own total uselessness, and Xerxes shrank from Joey's common-cat activities, like stalking rodents. There was only one trick around the house that they seemed to share and, even with that, Joey mostly competed against Xerxes to show that anything he did, she could do better.

Xerxes put his trick into play when That Man sat down to read in his armchair in the living room. The cat crept in behind That Man and lay there silently until he was forgotten about. Then without warning, he leaped from behind out of nowhere, right up on his shoulder. This had a startling effect on That Man. The first couple of times Xerxes did it, That Man rose up abruptly from his chair and stood with his hand monitoring his heart, while Xerxes clung onto his shoulder and purred at full volume into his ear.

When That Man took him in his hands to put him back down

on the floor, Xerxes would scramble to stay up, showing a wholly uncharacteristic energy and determination, until That Man held him on his side with both hands and played him like an accordion, just as he did with Joey, stretching him out and compressing him, back and forth, until Xerxes was content to return to the floor. Xerxes's trick always worked in turning him into an accordion, and he told us, "No, I don't believe in slavery—my goodness, of course not. But it certainly is pleasant to have a human who does what I want every time I tell him to."

Meanwhile, after Joey had watched him doing that trick a few times, she said, "You think that's clever, do you, Herpes? Well, just watch me the next time That Man sits down to read the paper."

On schedule, Joey manoeuvred around That Man unseen until she was behind him. Then she made a mighty leap, not onto his shoulder, but right over it, and crashed into the newspaper he was holding. The paper jerked out of his hands, landing on his lap with Joey on top of it. Then she lay there and refused to move until That Man recovered from his shock and played her like an accordion, too. Xerxes's appraisal was that both tricks were excellent; Joey's was just a bit flashier, that was all.

I was taking a nap in front of That Man one time when I was awakened by the now-familiar sound of a cat crashing onto his newspaper. As Joey settled down on top of it on his lap, I asked her, "What have you got against That Man reading? You do the same thing up in the attic, lying on top of his sheets when he tries to read them. Why?"

"What? Haven't you noticed? He's a bossy know-it-all, Dork."

"Yes, if I didn't love him dearly I'd say he's all of that, and more. But what's that got to do with you jumping on top of his papers every chance you get?"

"You'd do it, too, if you could, Dork, but you can't because you ruined your chances at lap-leaping by hopping up on Granny's that time and half-drowning her with wine."

"If you'd been there to see it, instead of going by That Man's hearsay, you'd realize that it was a complete misunderstanding. I was only a puppy."

"Right. A sixty-pound puppy. You were nearly as heavy as Herpes over there."

Xerxes cut in to defend his honour. "Comparing Durf's weight with mine is inappropriate, Joella. Nice Girl weighed me yesterday and I barely hit the fourteen-pound mark. She even called me a wee slip of a thing. Although I was surprised when she wondered if I was getting extra food to eat somewhere."

I had a moment of panic. "You didn't let on about the big bag of beef jerky I found down in the basement, did you? That Man was keeping it for his next fishing trip, and I'm counting on him not discovering the empty bag till the morning he's leaving, so I'll know when to make myself scarce."

"Or that I let you eat my cat food half the time," said Joey, "because I'm already filled up from my hunting expeditions outdoors?"

"No, no, I just waved my tail, and she said it must be all this beautiful fluffy fur I have that makes me seem to be a little bit chubby." Xerxes puckered up in case Joey came over and cuffed him for mentioning his beautiful fur yet again.

But I got her back on point. "Joey, what has the fact that you lie down on top of That Man's papers got to do with his bossy reign of terror?"

"It stops him from reading about more old stuff to preach at us and order us around with."

I was staggered by the depth of her brilliance. It hurt me to say it to a cat, but I had to utter the simple truth: "Joey, you are a genius."

"Thanks, Dork. Coming from someone who's nearly as smart as Herpes, that's a real compliment."

"Oh, I'd say Durf is every bit as intelligent as I am, Joella," said Xerxes. "He just hides it better by acting so stupid."

"Thank you, Xerxes," I said. "You know, guys, with all this brainpower we possess, the three of us should get together to take on That Man and force him to cut back on his high-handed ways. The way we let him divide and rule us now is ridiculous."

"I was thinking the same thing, Dork," said Joey. "I have another trick that I sometimes play on That Man by myself. It worked pretty well the first time or two—really rattled the guy—but now it's starting to run out of steam. But if you and Herpes would team up with me on it, we could build up the terror and frighten Mr. Big Boots to death with it, or at least drive him insane."

I was delighted at the invitation and agreed to plan out the scenario with the other two and rehearse it to perfection. Then we waited for our opportunity, which was a night when Nice Woman was away and the kids were out having sleepovers, and That Man was alone in the house.

That Man lounged in his chair to read as usual, and Joey and Xerxes rambled into the room and sat close together a few feet in front of him. Then I moseyed casually in and lay down on the floor behind the two cats, all of us facing toward That Man and staring fixedly at the same spot behind him with worried eyes. When That Man noticed our riveted, anxious stare, he looked behind him. Seeing nothing, he just shifted uncomfortably and went back reading. He'd been through this routine before with

Joey alone, and nothing ever came of it but a few momentary goosebumps.

But with the three of us involved this time, we hoped to escalate the horror. We kept right on staring at the same spot. Then, when That Man looked at us again, I elevated my ears in alarm, and we all shifted our heads, slowly and completely in unison toward him, as if we were following with fearful eyes the movement of something hideous behind him. Our eyes stopped at the same instant and gazed in ever-growing dread at an identical point right over his shoulder.

That Man rose smartly from his chair and twisted around to see whatever it was our six eyes were trained on in such dread. Observing nothing, he turned back to us, only to see Joey and Xerxes scrambling in utter panic from the room, meowing and bumping and jostling at the door in their desperation to get out. At the same time, I jumped to my feet, emitted a yelp, and clambered out the door with the two cats, all of us tangled up in each other in our stampede to get away from the ghastliness still inside the room with That Man.

With his head swivelling like a weather vane to look all around, he slowly crept sideways across the room, and then backed out through the doorway. Staring in from the hall at the vacant but somehow horrifying point above his chair, he kept asking us, "What was it? What did you see?" He received in reply our six wide-open eyes gawping through the doorway in horror, and the cats' anxiously agitated tails and arched backs, plus my raised hackles.

He crept in a spiral motion into the kitchen and sat at the table, his back to the corner. There, he tried to read his book, but he acted extremely unsettled for the rest of the night, and his eyes constantly darted about, monitoring the empty air around him.

Out of his view, Joey, Xerxes, and I low-fived each other over our success. (I found high-fiving too hard.) Our team project to unhinge That Man had worked like a charm.

That night at bedtime, That Man called me to walk up to his bedroom with him. In Nice Woman's absence, he was sleeping alone. Up there he said, "Durf, you can bunk down in here tonight as a special treat." It was a special treat, all right, but not the one he pretended he was giving me. The treat was that he was on his knees begging for my protection. He'd been forced at last to give up trying to usurp the alpha position, and now had to occupy his true beta rank, relying on my leadership, and acting as my second-in-command, and beseeching me for my protection. Oh, I loved That Man dearly, of course, so I was overjoyed that he'd finally realized I would love him more if he just stayed in number two position under my unchallenged security and guidance. The world had righted itself at last.

The only thing wrong with the scene was Joey sitting just outside the bedroom door beside Xerxes, looking in at me. She was grooming herself with an insufferable expression of superiority, for some reason. "Whenever there's anything you can't handle in your 'leadership' position, Dork," she said, making sarcastic scare quotes with her paw, "just let me know and I'll straighten it out for you." She was out there taking credit for my meteoric rise to the top!

Xerxes confirmed it: "You're really lucky to have Joella as your guru, Durf. Whenever you get in over your head, which I can't help noticing is most of the time, she's always there to guide you in the right direction."

Oh, this was great! Here I was, top dog for five minutes, and already I had to fend off a blatant takeover bid—no, an all-out bloodless coup—by the two cats in league with each other. Historians of the future, who may claim that I was not one hundred per cent successful in taking and maintaining complete control of my household all the time, will need to remember that, with That Man on the one hand and those cats on the other, I was constantly waging a struggle on two fronts—the downfall of many a lesser leader.

Chapter 11

The Stoop-and-Scoop Catastrophe

Nice Boy and I went for a walk on the sidewalks together nearly every day after supper, summer and winter. I loved it. We were buddies, and although we were linked together by a leash, there was no pressure or competition, and we saw eye to eye on where I roamed or stopped for a sniff or to mark territory.

On top of that, as That Man's leader I took him for a hike, three or four times a week during lunchtime, up on Signal Hill. It was child's play for me to motivate him to come hiking every time I wanted. All I had to do was bounce about the house, pretending I was off my head. That would make him say that I had to burn off more energy. If my excess energy was not expended, he'd read somewhere, it would come out in undesirable ways. "And I don't want to find out what could possibly be more undesirable than now," he kidded. "Come on, Durf, let's go."

Early on, when we went up on the Hill, we were not leashed together and both of us could roam around free. So, on every hike

I aimed to do three things religiously, or, according to That Man, "satanically."

My first order of business was the pizza miracle. No matter where else we wandered, I had to scramble an extra half-mile down to the end of the Burma Road, to a specific spot, a square foot on Cuckold's Cove Road, just up from Quidi Vidi Battery. It was there, on our very first walk, that the miracle had occurred: I found a pizza box, right in the middle of the road, with more than half a large pizza still in it. That Man kept shouting as he laboured to catch up with me, "No Durf, stop Durf, bad Durf." But before he could reach me, I had eaten it all. It's always hard to put on your stop-gorging brakes if you never know when bears or wolves or packs of hyenas are going to appear out of nowhere and muscle your meal away from you.

That Man picked up the box before I could lick it clean, and he was so contrary that, instead of licking it clean himself, he threw it in a garbage bin. Every time after that, whenever we went for a walk, I always ran down to exactly the same place to eat the next pizza that I just knew would be miraculously lying there on the ground. But there never was another one.

I was disappointed, but I kept the faith. Its absence made no difference to my quest. Each day on our hike, I believed fervently there would be another pizza there—the nature of miracles was that they came out of the blue when they felt like it, not when you wanted them to happen. I just had to have true conviction, and be there for the next miracle pizza when it did happen, that was all.

Even That Man was impressed by my devotion. "Durfy, what kind of a memory do you have on you at all," he said months later, when I ran down to the miracle spot. Afterwards, when we were leashed together, I had to become a martyr to my belief, because he of little faith always said, without even looking, "There's no pizza there, Durf; we're not going down there." And he'd stubbornly refuse to walk that measly half-mile off our path, and back. Every frustrating time that happened, I underwent a terrible minute of intense miracle-deprived suffering and martyrdom.

The second thing I had to do on our walks was frighten That Man out of his wits by plunging off a cliff. At least, I gave him the impression I was plunging, by picking my way down a steep rock face, whenever one presented itself, and disappearing into the clinging brush. The cliff that was halfway up the trail to Ladies' Lookout was one of the best, and That Man welcomed me back with many pats and ear rubs when I climbed up again. "My heart is in my throat," he'd say, "whenever I see you going down there." It was very gratifying to know that I could scare him back in line. But that all ended the afternoon I smelled unusual wildlife in the air and saw two big birds soaring overhead.

"Bald eagles," said That Man, gazing down at their nest on the top of a gnarled tree in the valley. "And they have eaglets in their aerie." Being so interested in nature, I took off down over the side of the cliff just to have a closer look and a good sniff, ignoring That Man's shouts of "Come back, Durf, you'll be killed." I can say with virtual certainty that, contrary to Joey's allegation later, I had no intention of snacking on those eagle chicks. However, I didn't get a chance to prove my good intentions. Suddenly, without warning, the sun was blotted out of the sky by wide, beating wings, and I felt something sharp digging into my head, neck, and back.

I was being brutally attacked from the air by two great big birds; they were dive-bombing me without provocation and without mercy, and seizing my fur and skin in their needle-sharp talons and ferocious beaks. Oh, I agree it was wonderful that mommy and daddy eagle thought they were protecting their young ones, but listen, those scraggly little chicks were certainly not cute enough for them to half kill me like that.

I rocketed up out of there to where That Man was waiting. He took one look at me and said, "We've got to get you to the vet. In the name of heavens, Durf, what is wrong with you? Where's your brain?"

Check with those eagles you dragged me to, I thought. *I'd say they have it.* I sulked all the way to the clinic.

Luckily, my vet cheered me up with her positive attitude: "I'm learning more from your visits, Durf, than I did at vet college."

When I arrived home, Joey examined my wounds, showing more fascination than distress. She became enthralled with the eagles. Questions galore! How long were their talons? Were they longer than her own claws? How sharp were they? I described them and told her she sounded jealous.

"Jealous?" she said. "I guess so! Who wouldn't be jealous of claws that can make mincemeat like that out of a big hulking brute?" Xerxes whispered to me later that Joey was considering having claw-enlargement surgery done.

After the kids got home and examined my wounds, Nice Boy said that, in view of how adventurous and courageous I was, he was going to make some serious inquiries about body armour for dogs, for every time I went out the door. See? The practical approach.

Following that day, during every walk we took on Signal Hill, That Man went up the trail to look down at the eagle's nest with his binoculars. Up there, I lay down on the ground tight to his leg. It was sufficient that I'd already seen the nest once, and being a strong nature conservationist, of course, I had no desire to disrupt the lives of that family of birds by going anywhere near them again.

The third thing I wanted to do, during our hikes on the Hill, was leap into a big bog. When I did it, That Man stood on the bank, watching me cavorting about, his eyes wide with admiration, I thought, and his lips moving soundlessly, drowned out by my splashes, but no doubt cheering me on.

When I came out, I had a beautiful coat of mud and gunk on my legs, belly, and halfway up my sides, and I smelled to high heavens, just the way I liked it. It was such a good bog that most of the muck wouldn't come off me, despite the three good shakes I gave my fur. Even That Man was impressed—no small achievement. He said he couldn't believe the mess, and that I could not get in the car like that. We'd have to leave it parked at the visitors' information centre and walk all the way home.

That was the right decision because, on the way back, people passing us admired my fabulous caking of mud and decayed peat. At home, That Man took me out to the backyard and turned the hose on me. Then he had to phone a taxi to drive him back up Signal Hill to get his car so that he could finally go to the office that afternoon, late for an appointment. "When you've succeeded in bankrupting me, Durf," he said before he left, "I hope we can get a good price for you at the sale of assets."

Joey, who was inside with Xerxes watching the activities in the backyard through a screen window, called out to me, "I'd say that when buyers become fully aware of your talents, Dorko, you'll bring in ten thousand bucks, easy."

"Oh, I'd say even more than that," said Xerxes. "Nice Boy and Nice Girl believe Durf is a highly superior dog."

I had no doubt the cats were being conservative about my

price range, but my ever-present modesty kicked in as usual. If I have a fault, which I don't, it would be that I'm perhaps a little too modest. So I was forced to say, "Very flattering, you guys, but I'd be mildly surprised if a willing buyer paid a whole lot more than ten grand for me."

Joey stared out at me for a while, with an amazed look on her face. Then she muttered to herself, "He took me serious. He really thinks . . . I need to go and have a nap."

When the kids, later that evening, heard about my frolic in the bog, they said they were sorry they'd missed all the fun. That Man told them he was pretty sure there'd be other opportunities for more "fun with Durf." Sometimes the guy could be okay.

Before long, though, That Man and I were leashed together like a chain gang for our walks on Signal Hill. True, he'd become strangely obsessed with keeping me out of the bogs, but that was by no means the whole reason for our change from freedom to captivity.

The main reason for our leash was a reaction from some people who went up there and considered the shrubs, brush, bogs, and rock of the National Historic Site to be a manicured urban garden and way too elegant to be left to nature alone. They complained to management about my carefree ways, especially regarding the call of nature. Sometimes, when I felt that call and had to perform my natural number two business, I went into the underbrush. Now and then, though, I performed the ritual on a trail, but that was okay because, in those cases, That Man enjoyed picking it up with a plastic bag. He always ran over and gathered it quickly and then carried it around with him for a good while like the crown jewels. I was happy to be able to oblige him.

One day on the hill, as I approached a crowd of hikers coming our way, I felt a strong call of nature and did my business in the middle of the trail. One of the hikers saw me in a squat and said, "My God, look what that Lab is doing right where we're going." Then I heard, "Oh, peeugh!" and, "How disgusting!" and, "Ugh, what a hum!" Talk about urban softies. And how was I supposed to know that the stiff breeze was blowing from me and my business directly at them? What did they take me for, a canine windsock?

Surprisingly, That Man's reaction seemed to be a little over-the-top, too, for a nature enthusiast. "Oh no," he groaned as he came running up. "Durf, what did you do that right there for? On today of all days?" It was almost as if he didn't grasp that I'd done it right there to make his life easier.

One hiker asked, "Did you say he was a Lab? Can't be. Labs are supposed to be intelligent and clean." Well, smarty-pants, Labs can have hurt feelings, too, you know.

That Man said to them, "Look, I'm sorry but I forgot to bring my stoop-and-scoop bags with me today. I'll find something to clean it up with."

"Well, you'd better get rid of it somehow," said a hiker. "There are signs all over this National Historic Site about dog owners' responsibilities when it comes to fouling the trails. I've already discussed this with the superintendent, and she says that irresponsible dogs and owners who do not follow the rules will be banned from the site."

"I agree," said That Man. "I've often complained about dogs and humans who leave a mess behind, myself." He whipped off his nylon windbreaker, used it in place of a plastic bag, and carefully rolled it up around the contents. The hikers protested that that was certainly a desperate measure. Now they were complaining about how ingeniously my second-in-command had solved their big "crisis." Good heavens—humans! But That Man seemed just as bad. The expression on his face, when he dumped the works into the first garbage can he came to, showed a subordinate who looked almost mutinous, if not murderous.

From then on, to satisfy the soul-destroying official rules on all our walks, he and I were yoked together with a leash. Any time I felt an urge to do my natural business, I barely had time to hunker down to the ground before I felt myself yanked into the bush, where, to be frank, the branches made it not nearly so comfortable as the middle of the trail. And him standing there with a pocketful of fresh stoop-and-scoop bags he could have used! I could no longer deny the unmistakable: That Man was going more and more rebellious on me.

As a result of that leash when I led That Man along the trails, I had to forgo my headlong nosedives over cliffs, and my hope of a lovely, cool, smelly, mud-bespattered romp in the bog, and my faithful quest of the coming pizza miracle. The two of us moved nearly as slowly as when I was running with Zippo the sausage.

But our trudges side by side turned out to be inspiring each time. That Man and I used our forced togetherness to talk about the many riveting and captivating events in my life—all the ups and downs with the grown-ups and kids and cats and dogs. Now, I'm not holding my breath, but if he writes down the truth, which he promised he'd do, then I agree with what he told me: my tale will be an inspiration to the whole of humankind.

Chapter 12

I Rescue That Man, Whether He Needed It or Not

As the old name for my breed, water dog, hints, I love the water. I love jumping in, swimming around forever, and retrieving things and bringing them back to shore. I remember how impressed my whole family was one day when we were having a picnic at a table beside the Exploits River. I saw a big piece of wood floating by quickly, too good to resist. I bounded away from our picnic and leaped into the river. As I swam out to it, the closer I got, the bigger the log became. Reaching it, I tried many times before I was finally able to grasp some bark with my front teeth. Now I only had to bring it in to my family on shore.

When I looked for them, a scare went through me. I had drifted downstream so far I could barely see them way up on the bank of the river. Nevertheless, I set out, swimming with all my might. I got nowhere and stayed in one spot. Part of the problem was that I was pushing the log broadside to the current. But I found that if I went right to the narrow end and held that between my jaws, the thick end flowed back and the log went through the water like a spear. Now I was making some headway, but progress was still slow and hard going. It was taking me so long to swim back that my whole family was edging down the riverbank and shouting: "Let go of the log, Durf, and swim in," "Drop the log, my pup, and come back to shore," and similar defeatism and despair, or common sense, unfamiliar to my kind.

"No way!" I said to myself, even as exhaustion started to overtake me. "I've got that darn log in my teeth, and that darn log is going in with me." I kept paddling and paddling, and I don't know how I did it, but at last I made it to shore, only a short distance below the picnic table. I was so tired I just stood there in water up to the top of my legs, all parts of me trembling like aspen leaves, with the end of the log still in my mouth and the rest of it floating in the water. I would not let it go for anything.

Nice Boy and That Man waded out and helped me tow the log onto dry land. It was so heavy out of the water that it took the strength of the three of us to drag it onto the beach, where we dropped it. Nice Woman and Nice Girl joined the other two in praising me for being "really good at swimming out to stuff" and bringing it ashore.

"Okay," said That Man, "now that we have this log, what do we do with it?"

Do with it? What was he talking about? What did doing something with it have to do with me? I'd retrieved it and my exploit had been noted and praised; I'd done all the good I could in these parts. My work here was done. I ran back up to the barbecue to be close by for when the next batch of hamburgers was cooked.

My success in retrieving a log from a deep, fast-flowing river, and the appreciation of all who saw the feat, made me start to dream about being a hero. I visualized day and night a big ship sinking, throwing hundreds of passengers into the ocean, and me swimming out to them and bringing every single one of them in to shore, safe and sound. The greatest rescue in the history of the world. I was dying for that to happen so that I could prove to humans and animals worldwide, especially Joey and Xerxes and That Man, the three who seemed the most skeptical, what a clever dog they had the honour of rubbing shoulders with.

I waited and waited for my expected big ship to sink, and I never gave up hope of being a superhero. Then, one afternoon, a little bit of my wish was granted, sort of a practice session for the real thing: I rescued That Man from drowning. Full disclosure: there were divided opinions on the "drowning" part of the rescue. I knew he was drowning, but he claimed he wasn't. Most likely he was too big-headed to admit I had to save him. That Man's pride will be the end of him one day.

On the day in question, he was goofing around with the kids in Granny's and Grampy's swimming pool at their cottage, and I was lying in the sun nearby, dropping off into a little nap. In my dream, as usual, the ship was sinking, and I was just swimming out to rescue the passengers, when a shout from one of the kids woke me up. I saw That Man in the deep end, treading water and talking to Nice Boy and Nice Girl, who were now standing on the deck. That was strange: usually he got out of the pool first, while they stayed in, playing. I don't know how I knew it—call it unerring canine intuition similar to when a dog will sense that an earthquake is about to strike—but the realization suddenly came to me that he was drowning and urgently needed to be retrieved from the water.

"Without hesitation and with total disregard for his own safety . . ." as I knew my bravery citation would read, I jumped up and ran toward the pool and flew right in, all four webbed paws spread forward and backward in perfect form. Then I made for my drowning victim, dog-paddling furiously.

Hearing my splash, That Man turned around in the water. He must have seen, of course, that I was about to rescue him, but instead of saying "Good Durf, good boy," he started yelling, "No Durf, no." That was his confused state of mind from drowning at work. I reached him in seconds, but he didn't hold on to me and let me save him. In fact, he wouldn't co-operate at all, but kept pushing me off. I had no choice but to climb up on top of him to calm him down. Still he fought me, even when I put my paws on his head and shoved him underwater to show him I was in charge of this emergency.

When he came up again, I approached him from behind and got up on his shoulders. You'd think that anyone mature and sensible, as That Man always pretended to be, would relax and grab hold of me and let me swim to the side of the pool with him in tow. But oh no. That wasn't contrary and unco-operative enough to suit him. The whole while I was rescuing him, he kept roaring, "Get off me, Durf, you numbskull." Distress makes a person say strange things.

Then he went underwater, causing me to flounder around in anxiety for his safety, but somehow he struggled to the side of the pool by himself—pure dumb luck—and surfaced and hoisted himself out of the water. How silly he'd acted was seen from the fact that Nice Woman and Nice Boy and Nice Girl, and some cousins sitting around the pool, were all laughing their heads off. It was odd, though, how fast the situation went from laughable to tragic.

When I went over to hoist myself out of the pool, too, I suddenly realized that I couldn't do it. Somehow, whoever had built this pool had constructed the walls so that a dog couldn't get out. I put my front paws on top of the side of the pool, but they wouldn't stay there. They kept sliding off and down into the water again. I swam around looking for steps I could walk up over or some other way out of the pool. But there was nothing, only two little metal ladders, impossible to climb.

It came to me in a flash of panic that the pool had been deliberately constructed to kill me. This was a fiendish plot. Before I'd jumped in I'd never given a thought to how to get out. I'd seen adults and kids pull themselves up over the side with ease, so why couldn't I do the same? But now it was evident that my enemies had cunningly concealed from my eyes the full diabolical nature of the pool until it was too late. Dangerous though my situation was, I still had time to wonder if cats were somehow behind the construction of this sinister dog trap. And I quickly concluded it was so evil that, yes, they had to be. If I survived, which was more doubtful by the second, I made a mental note-to-self to conduct a third-degree interrogation of Joey the cat conspirator to corroborate that felines were behind this treacherous plot.

I swam around the sides, barking out a simple instruction to That Man, "Drain the pool, drain the pool." But he couldn't even do that. In fact, he did nothing but continue to dry himself, slow and unconcerned, not even looking at me. It was becoming very clear to me now that he was either a co-conspirator or a moron. At last, he placed his towel around his neck and walked at a snail's pace over to where I was scrambling vainly to get out. "Do you need a little help, Durfy?" he asked sweetly. What was he, blind, on top of wicked and stupid?

By now Nice Boy and Nice Girl and Nice Woman were leaning over the pool saying, "We've got to pull him out."

"Why on earth," That Man replied, "would we do that?"

The kids shouted at him, "Not funny, Dad!" What kind of father would "joke" to his own children about a brutal tragedy unfolding before their very eyes?

Now, finally, unhurriedly and reluctantly, he muttered, "Well, I suppose we'll have to. We can't have the swimming pool cluttered up with dead dogs." He reached down and grabbed my collar, while Nice Boy and Nice Girl took me under my front legs. They pulled at me, and That Man said, "Good heavens, what a weight. He was heavy enough dry, let alone wet." And here was I, doing all the heavy work with my front and hind paws skilfully clambering and scrambling against the side a mile a minute.

Once on the deck, I needed to shake the water off my fur. My coat is so ingeniously designed that, when I agitate it, the skin moves loose and fast, back and forth, all over my body, and catapults the water away with such force that it travels twenty feet in every direction. Nice Boy and Nice Girl laughed when the water hit them, and even That Man chuckled under protest as Nice Woman showed her superior intelligence, as usual, by ducking behind him before the drenching shower came their way. Everything had returned to happy-family normal, with me as the centre of attention. But what I hadn't realized was that just as I'd been about to let loose with the water explosion, Granny and Grampy and Zippo the sausage were approaching us from the side.

Granny and Grampy wanted to say goodbye before leaving for the Government House garden party, and they were wearing their spiffy smart-casual outfits. My only memory now of the scene was water dripping from Granny's sodden hairdo and her saturated frock, before the look on her face and her shrieked words, still surprisingly feisty for a kind-hearted woman in her sunset years, triggered a reflex action in me. I took off out the gate and into the deep woods. I wasn't sure if my instinct to flee was correct or not, because Zippo followed behind me barking out mixed signals: "Durf, Granny wants you to come back." I stopped to hear more. "She says she's going to murder you."

After that afternoon, I never dreamed again, day or night, of the sinking ship or of becoming the big hero of the ocean rescue. Having saved That Man, and then myself, under the most trying circumstances, I figured I'd performed enough watery heroics for one lifetime. But still, in the back of my mind, I couldn't help believing that fate, somehow, somewhere, had great glory in store for me.

What I couldn't foresee then was that I hadn't yet hit bottom in my quest for hero status; because, soon after that, instead of achieving the triumph and glory I sought, I became a villain.

Chapter 13

Monster and Moose

I certainly didn't intend to be as evil as everyone thought I was. When I was telling the cats later about the trouble I got into, Joey summed it up this way: "One good thing about being a nincompoop, Dork, is that you don't have to work very hard at becoming a baddie: it just happens."

Well, this happened on the Labour Day weekend in Gros Morne National Park, our last outing before Nice Boy and Nice Girl went back to school. My family and I, except for the cats, were staying at a cabin there. Xerxes and Joey had to be left home with a sitter because, as That Man said, "I'd love them to come, too, kids, but think of the logistics of hiking with a couple of cats?" So that was good—the cats being put in their rightful place compared to a dog. But it was bad, too, because I could have used their company during the part of the trip when everyone hated me.

We were at a campground cooking wieners, and lots of kids were using the playground equipment. Nice Boy and Nice Girl had made some friends, especially a little girl younger than them, who was very lively and cute. They took her under their wing and, therefore, of course, I included her with them as under my protection. Suddenly, when I looked away for a moment from the cooking wieners to the young ones, I saw something scary happening.

The little girl was being captured by a monster! It was taking her high in the air, while her father behind her was trying to rescue her. Without thinking, I took off straight for them and sank my teeth into the monster that had seized her. Chaos broke out. The little girl started to wail, and her father started to roar, and he grabbed me by the collar, pulled me away, and kicked me in the ribs. But, as a result of my actions, I thought, the little girl's mother was able to rescue her from the monster by picking her up and holding her in her arms, so I didn't know why there was such a hostile fuss directed at me. I'd even been rejoicing to myself, "Mission accomplished," before I got the kick from the father. Then That Man pulled me by the collar away from the scene altogether, shouting "no" at me, and the girl's father yelled behind us that I was a menace and should be put down. What in the name of heavens, I could only wonder, was going on here?

It turned out to be a misunderstanding on both sides, simple but serious. Until that time, I wasn't familiar with kids in those big leather swings, and I thought the little girl in the swing was being captured and was going to be devoured. Although I was attacking the monster swing itself to rescue her, everyone else thought I was out of control and attacking the little girl. Her father threatened to sue my family and I was kept on a leash for the rest of the day and people were very distant with me. That Man was talking about leaving me in the cabin for the rest of the weekend, to be let out on the leash only for restroom breaks.

I was being wrongly accused, yes, but my family was so shocked and saddened by my actions, as they too had misunderstood them, that I could only lie around depressed and miserable. Whether I was innocent or guilty, if my family didn't love me anymore, that was enough: it could only be all my fault. I wished, as the little girl's father had shrieked, that someone would put me down. That sounded bad, whatever it was, but it still seemed too good for the likes of me.

When I told the cats about it later, Joey said, "Dork, I'm gathering here that you don't know what being 'put down' means." She'd learned all about the possibility of being put down, out at the barn, she said, before being rescued by Nice Girl.

After she explained to me what it meant, I said, "Well, that doesn't sound too good for me after all. I think I'd rather have something else that wouldn't be too good for me—a moose steak, say. I think that would be okay, especially after my run-in with that vicious bull moose that was attacking people."

"Oh, a bull moose, now, is it, Dorky?" said Joey, yawning. "This is gonna be good."

"Did you save the day this time," asked Xerxes, "or was it another disaster?"

"You tell me, Xerks. Because I can't tell if I'm a hero or a villain anymore."

The evening following the monster-swing calamity, my family relented on making me a prisoner. Under persuasion from Nice Boy and Nice Girl, they let me in the car to go on a drive with them. Leaving the cabin grounds, we saw the same little girl walking along the gravel driveway hand in hand with her mother. They were staying four or five cabins away from us. As we drove past them, That Man said, "Keep Durf out of sight," and opened his window to say, "Good evening." The mother didn't respond.

Nice Girl opened her window and called out the little girl's name and said, "Hi." I was looking at them fearfully from behind Nice Girl and saw the little girl wave back. But her mother made no eye contact with any of us in the car.

Then Nice Woman said, "Look at that over there. It's an enormous moose."

We all turned our eyes to where she was pointing. Loping out of the woods and heading toward us was a humongous animal. "Yes, it's a bull moose," said That Man, stopping the car. "Just look at the huge antlers on him. He doesn't look very happy, either. It must be nearly rutting season."

The woman and her daughter had their backs to the moose and, on those long, gangly legs, he was covering ground fast toward them. Nice Woman shouted out to the other woman to watch out, there was a moose behind them. The woman turned around and froze. In just seconds the moose had covered enough ground to be nearly upon her. That Man opened his door and stood outside the car, bellowing, "Run, over here, look out, this way, run, run!"

I could smell the moose's belligerent maleness wafting toward me on the air in great aggressive waves. That Man said later that he knew moose were not normally aggressive toward humans, unless it was a bull angered by something, or a cow finding someone standing between her and her calf. But this bull was clearly angered by something, and very aggressive, and was plainly about to attack the little girl and her mother.

I really don't recall what I did next. I was told later that I jumped cleanly out through Nice Girl's open window. All I knew was that the little girl I was responsible for protecting was in danger from this swift-paced beast that was approaching her and her mother. I ran past them and stood between them and the huge brute, barking and growling just as I'd done when I attacked the swing.

The moose slowed down and looked at me, and without pause he veered away from the mother and child and came barrelling my way, antlers down and hooves flashing. I ran around him, and his attention was once more taken by the mother and daughter; he moved toward them again. I was behind him now and sank my teeth into the back of his hind leg. He emitted a roar and turned around to lunge at me. He'd lost all interest in the humans now and concentrated his attention and strength on killing me. His front legs looked like spears as he thrust his hooves at me. I managed to evade his first two attempts to brain and disembowel me by jerking backwards and to the side.

I looked over at the little girl; her father had come out of their cabin and was now helping her and her mother away from the scene. That Man and Nice Boy were shouting at me, "Run, Durf, run away." That sounded like a really good idea, and I turned to run. But I had allowed my attention to shift away from the moose's hooves for a split second too long. I felt as if one of my hind legs was being torn from my body. When I looked, I saw that the moose's hoof had slashed off a swath of skin on my lower thigh, just above the joint, and the wound was gushing blood.

I managed to scramble away on three legs as the moose kept prancing ahead, trying to spear or trample me. It was only a matter of time, the way this was going, before he diced and mangled me into hamburger. Then I saw That Man's car coming toward us and nudging the rear end of the moose. He turned to his new target, lowered his head, and charged the car. His antlers made a good-sized dent in the grille. Next, evidently feeling that he had done as much good as he could to me and the car, he trotted off.

We saw now that he was moving toward his original adversary, another bull moose standing near the woods down the driveway, bellowing at him combatively.

My family and other people were standing around me, and I heard, "He's going to bleed to death," "We need a tourniquet," "Don't touch him, he's in pain, he'll tear your arm off," "Get a vet; is there a vet nearby?" The father of the little girl said, "There's a doctor in one of the cabins."

I was feeling weak now and lay down on my side. I heard, "No, don't put your hands on him, it's too dangerous." But Nice Boy said, "I don't care," and I felt my head being lifted onto his lap and his hands on my face and neck. I licked his hand. Then I heard a confident voice say, "That's good, you keep him still while I tranquilize him."

When I woke up I was lying on cushions in our cabin, with a tourniquet around my thigh and a bandage on my leg. Nice Boy and Nice Girl were sitting on the floor beside me and patting me. Then I saw the little girl and her mother and father sitting around the room, looking at me. When they saw that I was awake, everyone started saying, "Brave dog," "Durf the hero," and other words of praise far too numerous to mention.

Then the father and That Man started talking about moose. There were so many in the park, which was off limits to hunting, that it was getting way overcrowded, and bulls were becoming abnormally aggressive with everyone and everything in their competition for mates. And the danger they posed to people in vehicles driving on the roads was appalling. There was going to have to be a moose cull in the park. I certainly seconded the cull idea, starting with that bull today, and gave a woof of agreement. Everybody laughed. "Durf is all for that," said the father of the little girl. Then he stood up and said, "I hope he's going to be all right."

That Man said, "The doctor said he would be. We're just lucky he was around, because I don't think we would have been able to stop the bleeding."

The father of the little girl said, "And *we* were certainly lucky Durf was around. I shudder to think what might have happened to my wife and daughter if he wasn't."

The little girl said, "Can I pat him, Dad?" She got down with my kids and touched me gently on the head with her fingers. I lifted my head and gave her hand a little lick. "Good Durf," she said. "Good boy. We know that you weren't trying to hurt me on that swing after all, right Mom?"

"That's right, sweetheart," her mother said. "You didn't have a scratch or a mark on you. Good old Durf was a little bit confused and thought the swing was going to hurt you."

Telling Joey and Xerxes the story later, I added, "That was one smart lady, the way she figured out the swing mix-up."

"She couldn't have been all that smart, Dorky," said Joey, "if she said you were only 'a little bit' confused. Ha ha ha, just joking."

"I'm glad you said you were joking, Joella," said Xerxes in a stern voice, "because otherwise I'm afraid I would've been forced to take you on, verbally. Durf wasn't confused when he faced that moose, for sure, were you, Durf? You were brave and you deserved all the praise and compliments they gave you."

"Thank you, Xerks. I agree. But that wasn't the highlight of the adventure. That came the next day when I was by our car getting ready to drive back home. A great big black Newfoundland dog come up to me with his human and said, 'Good day, cousin Durf.' Imagine! I was amazed. A noble Newfoundland who knew my name.

"'Good day, your Excellency,' I answered, wondering what

his name was, but feeling too overawed to ask. I figured maybe 'Thunder' or 'Boomer,' because of his deep impressive bark, or perhaps 'Jupiter,' king of the dogs, because of his magnificent stature and bearing."

"Uh, Dork, wouldn't that be gods?" said Joey. "Jupiter was king of the gods, not the dogs."

"Gods, dogs, whatever," I said. "No need to split hairs, anyway, Joey. His name wasn't Jupiter. He said to me, 'My name is Twinkletoes. I am the head of our exalted clan of Newfoundlands and Labradors in Atlantic Canada, having been named Best in Show in Halifax last year. On behalf of our two related breeds, I congratulate you on your bravery. You have done us all proud by the way you so splendidly carried on our shared tradition of forever saving human beings left, right, and centre.'

"I thanked him and stood up in respect, in spite of my discomfort. He said, 'Uh, *Durf*, is it? What happened to your tail? The kink, I mean. That's really weird, dude.' Can you even imagine it? The chief of the noble breed from whose ancestors we had all descended saying, first, he was proud of me, and then noticing my tail. I can't believe it. What a story to tell my children and grandchildren."

"No problem finding them, Dorkums," said Joey. "You'll recognize them by their kinks."

"That was an extremely nice story," said Xerxes. "Really sweet. Twinkletoes. I think that's the best name I ever heard. I wish I had that name."

"But, unfortunately, if a top dog already has the name Twinkletoes," I said, "a cat can't use it. Protocol strictly forbids it."

"But what about if I change it to Twinkle-Furry-Between-Toes?"

"Hey, that might work. I'll ask Twinkletoes the next time I see him at a rescue celebration party."

"Oh lordy, I can't wait," said Xerxes.

Joey looked from me to Xerxes and back again three times with an expression of amazement on her face. "Herpes," she said, "to think I was going to ask you to join me in falling to our knees and thanking heaven we were born cats instead of dogs. But I see I'm too late. You're already halfway to becoming an honorary mutt."

"It's time we stopped this hostile segregation of the species of cats and dogs," said Xerxes, "and made the world one big happy place for all of us. Henceforth, I proclaim you and me, and even Durf, to be best friends. "

Joey had a lopsided grin on her face. "Oh my," she said to me. "He just makes you want to go over there and give him a great big kiss."

Chapter 14

Xerxes's Worst Nightmare

Before Christmas of the same year, That Man said to the family at dinner, "When it comes to Durf being a hero, it never rains but it pours. After years of being a bit a nuisance—no, not all the time, kids, that's not what I mean—but a little bit of a nuisance sometimes, you know, sort of, now and then? Now, suddenly, twice in a row—bang, bang—he's covered in fame and renown for saving the day once again."

He was talking about a recent rescue I'd done a little over three months after my moose adventure, which added to my big-headed vanity and conceit over becoming a legendary hero. Back then, I didn't think it was possible to receive too much glory and acclaim and admiration. And I loved every morsel of it. How could I have been so wrong?

What caused me to become so full of myself happened the night that Nice Boy and Nice Girl decided to have a pre-Christmas party at our house. The evening began with gently falling snow, unusually early, the first of the season. Lots of their friends arrived and everyone was having a terrific time, including me as I welcomed the kids into my house.

Nice Woman and That Man went upstairs, so as not to dampen their enjoyment, and watched television in the bedroom. Finally, I could no longer resist the new snow I saw piling up outside every time I greeted guests. My injury from the moose attack was all healed up by now, and I was raring to go. When one group of friends was coming in, I violated the rule against going outside without a leash and darted out into the winter night to frolic for half an hour in the white powder.

While I was out, I heard later, an older teenaged boy from school rang the doorbell. The partiers who answered the door saw immediately that he'd been drinking and wouldn't let him in. They told him to go away or they'd call the grown-ups. Nobody else even knew he'd been there, and the young fellow went staggering off into the frigid, snowy night.

Over an hour after I'd left—who was keeping time on a magnificent night like this?—I made my way back home, content with my wintery trek about the neighbourhood, and eager to join the fun again in the cozy house. The wind had come up and the snow was drifting heavily. I reached our driveway, but I never got to the back door.

That Man would say later that he heard me barking outside and looked out through an upstairs window. He saw me tugging at a garbage bag in the snow on a corner of our front lawn near the sidewalk. He came down, opened the front door, and asked me in a voice more irritated than he'd used for months, to please leave that garbage bag alone and come in right this minute. He figured I'd dragged the garbage bag back from somewhere, and he intended to wait till morning to ask

Nice Boy to dig it out of the snow and store it in the shed for next garbage day.

While he stood there calling me, I refused to come to him but just kept yanking at the "garbage bag." Finally, he decided he had to go out and get me, or otherwise I might tear the bag open and leave garbage strewn all over the place. Without disturbing the kids, he put on his boots and jacket and came out into the blowing snow, muttering unpleasantries at me the whole while. When he got to where I stood, he discovered what I had known all along: the dark shape nearly buried in the snow was not a garbage bag at all, but the drunk and now unconscious teenager.

That Man half carried, half dragged the boy into the house, where his appearance cast a pall of disquiet over the party. The two girls who with good intentions had sent him away from the door broke into tears. A couple of boys were kind enough to move close to them and console them. That Man and Nice Boy managed to bring the lad around somewhat, helped him upstairs, undressed him from his thawing outer garments, put him in a terry towel gown, wrapped him in blankets with a couple of hot water bottles, determined that he was somewhat lucid, and not dying, and lay him on his side in a bed to recover. That Man and I stayed in the room and watched him to make sure he kept breathing and didn't get sick.

At length he was able to get up and put on his now dry clothes. Then he went downstairs and had some laughs with his partying young friends about his "cool" escapade. That Man looked less than amused, though, as he marched him out to the taxi he'd ordered to deliver him home.

For days afterwards, family, relatives and friends heaped compliments on me for saving the young fellow from freezing to death on that frigid winter night. My head swelled up. I had saved the day, rescued yet another person, averted a human tragedy once again by doing things my way: I'd defied the ban on going outside without a leash and I'd brought into play my years of expertise with bags of garbage. Where were all their don'ts and their stops and their noes now? I was, without a pinch of doubt, the proud alpha male, inside the house and out.

All that spring, Joey begged Xerxes to go outside with him, again. The time had come to pick up where he'd left off last time, she kept saying. She seemed to be overdoing it with the pestering, if you asked me. Xerxes would look out the window at the wet, dirty snow lying around, or the freezing rain coming down sideways, and say, "Not right now, thank you, Joella. Perhaps later."

But when the weather got pleasant early in the summer, Xerxes said to Joey and me that she'd thought about it a lot, and my heroism with the bull moose and in saving the boy had inspired him. He was going to embark on a more thrill-seeking life himself. First of all, he wanted to get back at his outside orientation training, which had been disrupted before when he got lost on the lawn next door. He was all recovered from that traumatic ordeal now, he said, and felt up to cautiously exploring our own driveway and lawn, under my protection. Yes, the urge to adventure, he enthused, had come right over him with the warmer temperatures: my heroics had left him dreaming of nothing else. Would Joey and I, with our outdoor expertise and my protection, give him a hand and help to train him in?

Joey said she'd be happy to, just as long as Xerxes promised to go slow and easy and not try to take over as the top cat in town on the very first day.

"I promise, Joella. I'll let a couple of days go by before I even think about doing that."

I knew I should have said no to Xerxes. He'd been right all along: he just didn't have a clue when it came to navigating, or even surviving, outdoors. But he'd appealed to my vanity, bolstered by my feeling that I was capable of saving and protecting the whole world. So, I said, "Let's do it—the very next time someone leaves the door open long enough for us to make a break for it. And don't worry, Xerks, I'll guard you and defend you until you're on your feet out there."

Next garbage day, That Man carried out of the house four jam-packed recycling bags and pushed the door closed with his foot because his hands were full. It didn't catch and stayed open a crack. While he was at the side of the street talking to the man next door, I said, "Xerks, Joey, come on, let's make tracks. Follow me." We crept through the doorway, with Xerxes positioned between Joey and me, and snuck around the side of the shed, where we hid out of sight until That Man came back and went in the house.

"Good stuff, Xerky," I said. "How are you feeling so far?"

"Not too bad. A little jittery from all the excitement. But I'll be okay as soon as I get my bearings. Where's our house in relation to our present location?"

"It's around the corner about fifteen feet away. I'll show you as soon as everyone leaves."

"Meanwhile," said Joey, "Dork and I will stand guard over you, because you never know—with all that lovely blue fur, someone might take you for a polar bear, tranquilize you with a dart, hang you from a rope from a helicopter, and drop you off on an ice pack up by the North Pole."

"Heavens, I never thought of that," said Xerxes. "This is more hazardous than I expected. Okay, I think this has been enough for one day."

"I was joking, Herpes."

"No, you weren't, Joella. Dart me and hang me from a helicopter and drop me on the North Pole? You'd never joke about anything as serious as that. I'd like to go back in the house now, please."

"Shh, they're leaving."

All four family members rushed out of the house. The kids, thinking we were still inside, shouted back their goodbyes to us as they came through the door. They had their coats half on and were dragging their backpacks as they piled into the cars in a big hurry not to miss their drives to school.

There was no way, enjoying the outdoors like this, that Joey and I were going back in. "It's too late to get in the house anyway, Xerks," I said. "The whole family is gone."

"Mrs. Rock is still in there."

"Yeah, but she's so happy we're out of her way while she vacuums, she'll never let us in."

"You two, maybe. But I don't get in her way. The vacuum cleaner scares me so much, I always hide under the bed or the sofa farthest away from it. I'm going in. Show me the door so that I can meow at it."

I should have listened to him. Instead, I said. "You're not going to be taken for a polar bear, Xerxes. You yourself have always said that you don't want to go outside because your fur is so handsome someone might kidnap you. So, nobody is going to hang you from a helicopter as a polar bear. They'd be too busy kidnapping you."

"Yes, I did talk about the risk of someone carrying me off. And the family is always saying it. So it's true. Joella, I really wish you'd stop frightening me half to death all the time talking about me being taken for a polar bear. Okay, let's go exploring."

Joey, of course, in her relentless search for truth and logic, couldn't let Xerxes's reply go by. "Wait a sec, Herpes. Let me get this straight first. You were frightened to death you might be taken for a blue polar bear and hung from a helicopter and dumped at the North Pole, but now you're A-okay with the risk of being kidnapped."

The subtlety went over Xerxes's head. "What? You're mystifying me, Joella, with your 'you were this but now you're that.' Say it again."

"*Forgetaboutit*, Herp. Your mind is even more beautiful than your fur. Let's go. I'll show you where to stop at the edge of the street so that you don't wander out and get squashed into a pulp by a car."

Xerxes followed Joey, muttering, "What? Squashed into a pulp by a . . . ? Why didn't someone tell me it was a jungle out here? This outdoors place is a veritable minefield of death traps."

The three of us had just reached the sidewalk when Joey saw a pigeon landing on the grass back by the shed and instantly started slinking toward it. At nearly the same moment, I glimpsed that cute Samoyed, my lifelong soulmate to be, who lived way down the road, now on a leash, pulling her woman up the sidewalk toward me. Meanwhile, Xerxes was saying, "Okay, this much is probably adequate for one morning, Durf. I'd say we should head back to the house now."

I'd heard a dog on a cartoon show one time make a profound statement: "A dog's gotta do what a dog's gotta do." And it must have been true or they wouldn't have had it on TV. So I acted on it. I barked over my shoulder, "Talk later, Xerks," and ran down the street to greet my true love, the Samoyed. We only had time for a quick, mutually enjoyable sniff before her woman said to her, "Mrs. Amundsen, sit." Then she turned to me. "You! Get out of here. I told you that before." Oh well, the course of true love never did run smooth. I skilfully avoided the end of the leash, which I'd noticed last time had a surprisingly sharp sting, and ran back up toward our driveway.

I was halfway there when I saw a car stopping next to Xerxes. A man got out and picked him up. "My, you're a real beauty," he said. Then, seeing me coming, he walked back to the car fast. Hanging limply from the man's hands, Xerxes meowed loudly, "Durf, Joella, help me. It's my worst nightmare. I'm being hijacked." The man jumped into the car, and the woman behind the wheel sped away, squealing the tires.

I stood there flabbergasted. What did they do that for? I never saw either of them before in my life, and I'm sure Xerxes didn't know them, judging by his cry for help. I called out to Joey. She came trotting from the back of the shed, licking her lips. "Mmm," she said, "flying rat is right yummy."

"Are you talking about those city pigeons? I can never catch them. They're too wily. So I'm sure no cat can."

"Dork, I'd be surprised if a dog could catch a pumpkin growing in a field. So don't judge cats by yourself and your ilk. Listen, check out the bones behind the shed sometime to see what some cats can achieve. Nuff said. You'll have the Society for the Protection of Rats with Wings on me next. What were you just bawling out about?"

"Someone took Xerxes. A man and a woman took off in a car with him."

"No! Well, I'll be darned," said Joey. "Someone did kidnap him after all. Did they say anything—like why they would do such a senseless thing?"

"He said Xerxes was a real beauty."

"What?" Joey halted in her tracks and even stopped licking her lips. "I have to say I'm dumbfounded, Dork. Whenever Herpes said how beautiful he was, I thought he was being sarcastic and self-effacing. I mean to say . . . Herpes? A beauty? A cat that doesn't even look like a cat or act like a cat—bluish in colour, for heaven's sake, no nose, furry between toes, yellow eyes, can't hunt a housefly, in fact he's frightened of a housefly, gets lost out on our driveway, can't even keep his fur from becoming matted—a real beauty, Dorky? I mean to say, who knew?"

I was starting to get really upset as the disappearance of Xerxes on my watch sank in. I lashed out with blame: "Well, he's gone, and it's all your fault. You were behind the shed doing something unmentionable, instead of looking after him."

"My fault? I left you to babysit him, and next thing anyone knew you were down the street—I saw you—chatting up a dog who looked about as interested in you as she would be in a hippopotamus."

"She would have been if it wasn't for—what? You left me to babysit him? How was I supposed to know that? You're his fellow cat and you took off without a word."

"Oh, next time I'll holler out, 'Kindly excuse me, dear Dorky, I'm going to hunt that pigeon there that's listening to my every word and will now escape my clutches.' No wonder a dog is hopeless at stalking game."

I continued to try to wriggle out from under: "A dog babysit a cat? Are you gone cracked altogether? A dog doesn't babysit a cat. If I did that I'd be laughed out of the dump when word got around. It was you who was supposed to be looking after him."

"We're getting bogged down in quibbles here, Dork. What's done is done. No sense crying over spilled milk. Kitty Litter clumps happen. Can't be helped. *C'est la vie.* Time heals. It is what it is. Oh no: your hysteria has got me turned into a walking cliché. Let's look at this rationally. We'll soon get used to not having Herpes around. He wasn't what you'd call the life of the party anyway. Oh, sure, we'll mourn his absence for an appropriate period, and then move on. I'd say by tonight you and I will be back to normal again. Now, Nice Girl and the others, though . . . I have a feeling they're not going to like this. We'll just have to work at cheering them up, that's all."

Joey was trying to sound all valiant, but I could tell her reaction was only bravado and bluster, like mine. I clutched at straws: "Maybe the family won't even notice he's gone. When they come home, if you and I play dumb, maybe this will soon blow over."

"Play dumb? That might be a little easier for you to do than me, Dorky."

The back door opened and Mrs. Rock put her head out. "Durf, Joey," she shouted. "Oh, there you are. I was wondering where you took off to. I can't find Xerxes anywhere. Have you seen him?"

"Okay, act innocent," said Joey.

"Right, I'll carry on as if I'm normal."

"Don't attempt the impossible at this late stage, Dork. Just put on that face that gets you off with murder."

I made my best effort. "Don't give me that face, you skeet," said Mrs. Rock when I walked toward her. "It only proves you were up to no good. Where's Xerxes? He must've come out with you when you made a run for it again. And don't try to tell me he didn't. What have you two sleeveens got done with him? Oh my Lord, now I've got to call Mister or Missus and tell them Xerxes is lost or killed or something. And the children! Those precious little treasures are going to be heartbroken when they get home from school. I could beat the two faces off the pair of ya."

Mrs. Rock was right to be distraught, because when Nice Woman and Nice Girl and Nice Boy arrived home, they became heartsick and frantic at the absence of Xerxes. That Man tried to act the big hero as usual, strutting around spouting plans and directions like he was this massive tower of strength, but when Nice Girl said, with tears in her eyes, that she was afraid Xerky would never survive on his own out there, I saw a tear in his own eye as he was hugging his daughter. Behind his brave front, he obviously needed leadership so badly that I went up to him twice and licked his hand.

Over the next few days, the whole family made phone calls to neighbours and friends, walked about the neighbourhood knocking on doors, drove around streets searching everywhere, and put up "missing cat" posters on telephone poles and in stores, containing Nice Girl's favourite snap of Xerxes, and visited the city pound and the SPCA every day to see if he'd turned up. But there was no sign of Xerxes anywhere, and no one the family talked to had laid eyes on him.

"Not knowing is the worst," said Nice Woman to That Man. "Is he alive or dead? Did someone steal him, or heaven forbid, was he run over by a car? The kids are shattered by the thought of it all."

I'd thought from the start that I'd be a little sad he was gone. But I'd had no idea how much I'd actually miss him. Sometimes when I'd be lying on my stomach with my eyes closed, I felt as if Xerxes were lying there between my paws and reaching up and softly tapping my lip with his paw. But when I'd open my eyes to give him a little nuzzle, there was nothing between my paws but empty space. It was heart-rending. On top of that, I felt secretly responsible for what happened.

Joey was the biggest shocker to me. She walked around pretending to be her usual self, issuing rhetorical directives on how the household should feel: "Suck it up, all and sundry, Herpes is no longer in the building." Or, "Take comfort from the fact, everybody, that the bushy blue lunkhead is no longer lying belly up on the stairs, a menace to all humans." But her heart wasn't in it. That was clear from the way she just looked out the kitchen window at the pigeons and didn't even bother to scoot outside when someone opened the door. Neither did she seem to take much comfort from Nice Girl and Nice Boy picking her up more often than before and holding her longer. "Oh, I like it when they pamper me and everything, Dorky," she told me, "but I thought I'd be a lot happier than I am not having to share hug time with Herpes."

Then Joey confided to me that it was not so much that she missed Xerxes a little bit, but even worse, she felt guilty about his disappearance. She'd sometimes been jealous of him, she said, and she'd enticed him outside in the hope he'd get a good scare, maybe from a dog or a street cat, and have to turn to Joey for help, and then stop being so boastful afterwards about some of those admirable physical qualities of his. "But I had no idea, Dork, that this was going to happen," she said. "Or I definitely wouldn't have left you in charge."

I no longer protested. Instead, I said, "I feel guilty, too. I was so full of myself over being a big hero that I enticed him out with false promises of protection, and I let him down. Joey, you and I have got to do something."

"I know. There's no way around this, Dork. Our humans are driving me nuts with their moaning and groaning day and night. We've got to find him and bring him back here to shut them up."

"You're not fooling anyone with your tough talk, Joey," I said. "You don't miss Xerxes just a little bit. You miss him really, really bad, and that's all there is to it."

"Okay, okay, okay," said Joey, "I miss the big lug a lot, okay?" She clobbered me across the muzzle. "Happy now?"

"Let's go find him," I said, assuming my natural leadership role in the crisis. "Next time someone leaves the door open for a second, we'll go out and rescue Xerxes."

Chapter 15

Our Epic Rescue Attempt

Joey fell in with my rescue initiative. "Roger, Dork," she said. "But remember, the whole household is watching for our attempts to get out and trying to stop them. So wait for my all-clear signal so that we can slip out the door together in a rational and organized fashion."

I couldn't help thinking that everyone around here, except the sensible ones—Nice Woman and the two nice kids—wanted to be boss, whether they were equipped for the job or not, which they most definitely were not. If it wasn't That Man, it was Joey the cat trying to take over. One thing I'd always appreciated about Xerxes was that he had none of the delusions of grandeur those other two were afflicted with. He just assumed he was superior without having to constantly hit me over the head with it. It would be good to have him back.

We heard the key going in the lock. Someone was coming in. Joey started to creep stealthily toward the door. As it opened, I sort of forgot myself just a little and tore toward it. In the process,

Joey got tangled up in my feet and went flying to the side, and Nice Woman, about to come in, could only stand there speechless as I barrelled by her and out the door. Joey made it out, too, as a result of the diversion I'd created for her, and Nice Woman called out to the both of us to come back as we scampered down the driveway. But as much as it hurt me to pretend not to hear her, we couldn't stop because we were on a solemn quest to find Xerxes. We had to be cruel to be kind. We could not be sidetracked by anyone or anything.

Outside on the sidewalk, Joey was just saying, "You simpleton, you half-killed me," when I saw my only true love, the collie, jump out of her car. I started to run down the sidewalk toward her, but before I got very far, she and her man disappeared into the side door of her house. I stopped and sat down, stymied, and pondered my next move for the day. "Dork," said Joey, approaching and sitting down beside me, "What now?"

"What now what?"

"Herpes? Our missing—"

"Oh right, Xerxes. I knew there was something."

"What do we do now?"

"Well, what we do now is we find Xerxes and bring him back home."

"Good thinking," said Joey. "Guide us on our way, O maximus leader."

"Guide us on our way where? Why, where is he?"

"I haven't got a clue, Dork, but I figured you'd have a plan, what with those famous Labrador retriever sniffers, and your familiarity with all the streets from roaming around day and night following your dim and murky pursuits."

"Joey, this was all your idea. I'm the dog here and you're the cat. If anyone should know where a cat would be gone to, it would be another cat."

"But where do we even start, Dork? It looks like there's a lot of houses in this city. I think I heard That Man say one time there's nearly thirty thousand."

"Thirty thousand houses? No way. You must have heard wrong. Thirty houses, maybe. I've been beating around the city for a long time and I'm only acquainted with that many, max."

"You mean the houses where all the only true loves of your life live?"

"Right. But Xerks won't be at any of them. I'm familiar with the men and women in those houses, very close up, you might say, and that guy who took him, I never smelled or laid eyes on before."

"You mean you haven't got a clue where to go or how to get there." She sighed. "When Herpes disappeared I figured the average IQ in our house would go up. But I see now I was totally wrong. It's gone way down instead."

"Brain intelligence is not everything, Joey. Labs have a very high smelling intelligence, way higher than nearly every other animal."

Joey perked up. "You're picking up Herpes's scent?"

"No, not a trace."

"Oh, no." Joey groaned and flopped down on the sidewalk and closed her eyes in what looked like despair. "We haven't got a hope."

"Don't give up on me now, Joey. We'll just look for him and find him, that's all. Let's get going. It's the middle of the day now. If we hurry up we'll get him and bring him home in time for our supper."

I trotted up the sidewalk, taking charge. Pretending I knew

what I was doing made me feel like I knew what I was doing. The feeling was excellent. Joey came behind slowly at first, and then she caught up with me. "Dork, while you're looking at all the windows on this side, I'll look at the windows on the other side. Hopefully, sooner or later, we'll see Herpes looking out of one."

"Good strategic planning, Joey. I never thought of that."

"Well, how did you think we were going to . . . ?" She stopped and looked at me. Sometimes I wondered why Joey stared at me every now and then like I was an alien from another planet.

We trotted along, often crossing streets at intersections. I told Joey to stay right by my side, since I was bigger and used to this, and drivers could see me better than Joey. For the first time I could remember, Joey put up no argument to a suggestion of mine. All the traffic must have been scary to her, and she actually moved right in under me as she hurried to keep up. Once, a woman we passed said to the man with her, "Oh my heavens, how cute is that—a big dog and a little cat walking along together like buddies!"

"Don't go overboard, lady," said Joey. "Appearances can be deceiving. And did she say cute? Me forced by circumstances to be seen with a big galoot of a mutt?"

"Yes," I said, "I must say—buddies!—that was a bit much."

"We are merely partners of necessity here," said Joey. "Nothing more, nothing less."

"Dead-on," I said. I still felt happy as we walked along together, though, especially at the thought that I was protecting Joey from danger.

We kept going and going, looking at the windows of every house, moving straight ahead part of the time and turning right at intersections sometimes just for a change.

According to the doggy books that Nice Boy had read, a

Labrador retriever is *always* hungry. But I can confirm that those books were not true. From my own experience, a Lab is always *starving*. So I didn't mind the pangs of normal starvation I felt as Joey and I jogged along, since that was only an everyday sensation. But there's normal starvation and then there's famishing, wasting-away, terminal starvation. And what I started to feel now was that authentic starvation in the nature of a prolonged, unrelieved famine that could easily lead to the end of the world. That was because at least four hours had gone by since any food had passed my lips. I just knew I had gone past my suppertime, and by at least five minutes. The situation had become so dire that I was starting to hallucinate images of my feeding dish at home, piled high with mouth-watering yummies.

"Joey," I said, "I'm dying. You'll have to go on without me. Your mission is too important for me to interrupt or delay. Just leave me here in the gutter to perish."

"I knew it would come to this," said Joey. "You're gone ravenous on me, aren't you, Dork? You just want me to leave so that I won't see you ransacking someone's garbage bag and getting your rear end kicked again." I've never been able to figure out how Joey could read my mind all the time. Then she said something that proved that miracles can still happen in this modern day and age, despite the failure of the pizza miracle to come again: "Dork, isn't that our house over there?"

I looked, and sure enough, there it stood, across the street, our house. And, as if to allay all doubt, right there in front of the house, mowing the lawn, stood Nice Boy. When he spotted me, he turned off the lawn mower and I heard the best words ever uttered by a human being: "Come on, you guys, your supper is inside waiting for you."

I bounded across the street, causing a car to screech to a halt. Joey was so slow, she waited till the car was gone past before crossing. Nice Boy lowered the hand that he'd been covering his eyes with and said, "Durf, you're going to be killed yet. Why can't you be sensible crossing the street like Joey?" He grabbed me around the neck and hugged me hard. As he did so, I noticed that Joey took Nice Boy's compliment very seriously, or else she was lording it over me, judging by the way she sashayed across the street like a model on a runway, tail high in the air. I can't help remembering that image, years later, with a chill. Who could have guessed then what the future had in store for such a clever, careful cat?

Nice Girl came outside to greet us, too, and she knelt down to encourage Joey to jump into her arms. There, Joey purred nearly as loud as the lawn mower had just sounded. The kids asked where we had been and, of course, we had no idea. They told us not to disappear like that again. It worried them too much with Xerxes still on the missing list.

Inside at our feeding dishes, Joey said, "Dorky, tell me the truth. Do you have a certificate saying that you're a prizewinning champion nincompoop?"

"I'm not sure, Joey. I don't think so. I know my humans have certificates that I've had my shots. But I don't remember one saying I'm a prizewinning nincompoop. Why? Do you think I need one?"

"No, I don't, because it's absolutely clear without a certificate," said Joey. "But if you ever apply for one, just to hang on your wall, I'll back you up. There's lots of facts we can use. For instance, in our epic search for Herpes today, you led us around in one big circle, and you blundered back to exactly where you started from without even knowing it. That would be pretty good proof."

"Thanks, Joey. That did work out well. We were only a few minutes late for supper. If we can get out we'll search again tomorrow, and this time I'll make sure we blunder back to the house right on the dot." Joey gave me one of her speechless stares again. It was almost as if she couldn't believe that what she saw in front of her was real.

Chapter 16

I Become a Big TV Celebrity

Joey and I watched our chance, and we slipped outside together again. We were lucky we were able to do it when That Man was at the door. I couldn't bear to hear the distress in the voices of Nice Woman or the kids when they vainly tried to call us back.

We picked a direction and strolled along the sidewalk, having a good chat. We were really starting to bond. Xerxes would have been proud. Right away, Joey said, "So, Dork, let me guess. Our strategy for finding Herpes today is the same as yesterday: when you haven't got a plan, go around in circles."

"Right. My mother always said that the best way to get what you want is to go around and around. It's better than a straight line. Going around in circles, you have a much better chance of running into food opportunities, or the true love of your life, on the way. It's how our breed has survived and flourished, Mother said. It's hard-wired into us by forces of evolution."

"So, Dork, you remember your mother, do you?"

"My goodness, my sainted mother—of course I remember her, Joey. What do you expect?"

"What did she look like?"

"Er . . ."

"Did she look like a buffalo? Or did she look more like an orangutan?"

"You know, Joey, I never really noticed. We were too busy discussing search-and-find skills for food, and for me to get a nice proper girlfriend."

"Uh huh. Well, did you happen to notice if she was a boy dog or a girl dog?"

"Let's see . . . off the top of my head I'd say she was . . . er . . . Listen, Joey, this conversation is so interesting it's going to sidetrack us from our quest. We have to move faster and concentrate on locating Xerxes, or we'll never find him and get back to supper on time."

Joey muttered, "Back to supper on time! I'll be happy if we get back alive some day this year." She was certainly a pleasant travelling companion, making with the jokes all the time.

We walked and walked, looking in every window we saw, but again there was no sign of Xerxes. Then we came to a street where, on the other side, a gutter was overflowing with water gushing from a fire hydrant. Of course, I can't see water—puddle, stream, pond, or ocean—without having to get in it. So I ran over and jumped and frolicked about in this flow. I could hardly believe my good luck in coming across it. Joey walked over and stood there looking at me. "I thought we were in a hurry. I don't think you're going to find Herpes in there."

"No, but it's awful nice," I said. "Really refreshing on a hot day like this."

"Dork, it's about eight degrees out. I'm half-froze. Let's get going."

"Come on, put your tootsies in, Joey. Don't be a scaredy-cat."

Unlike Xerxes, Joey didn't like it one bit when she was labelled a scaredy-cat, because she most definitely wasn't one. The first time I'd called Joey that, Xerxes said, "You've got us mixed up, Durf. I'm the scaredy-cat. Joella is the bravest cat I've ever met in my life."

Instead of thanking him for the compliment, Joey had asked him, "How many cats have you ever met in your life, Herpes?"

And Xerxes replied, "Ah, let me think. One, I believe. Maybe I saw a couple in that shelter I was in. I can't remember."

"So, one cat, then. You mean me. And out of that sample, I'm the bravest cat you've ever met. Well, thank you, Herps, it's flattering to have my courage confirmed by an expert opinion." Joey's flippant attitude covered up her anxiety that others might think she was timid because she was only little. Her size didn't make her less brave, but it did make her cautious, and she wanted no one to confuse the two. Whenever I called her a scaredy-cat, she pretended to brush it off, but I noticed that it made her, if not foolhardy, then more prone to take a dare. I still feel guilty over taunting her on this day of the gushing hydrant.

In response, Joey leaned in and stretched one paw out into the swiftly streaming water. She misjudged the force of the flow and how slippery the asphalt was. Pulled off balance, she slid in. The depth and the speed of the water meant nothing to me. Even though it was halfway up my legs, I was heavy enough to stay stable in it. But Joey couldn't even reach bottom and was instantly swept away. All I could see was her head above the surface, very tiny-looking now that it was wet. She was paddling, trying to reach the side, but couldn't get a foothold.

I got out of the water and ran alongside her. I suddenly saw, farther down the street, that the cover had been removed from a manhole, and the torrent was plummeting into it. Joey was heading straight for that black hole and was going to disappear down into it and never be seen or heard from again. I barked at her to swim harder. Two men were across the street from the hydrant, one lifting tools out of their truck, and the other holding a big camera. They turned and saw us, but they were too far away to rescue Joey in time.

The manhole was now in plain sight for Joey to see, or else she could hear the roar of the waterfall, because she meowed, "Durf, please save me." Oh sure, now that she was in mortal danger, she was suddenly using my right name. But I didn't spend too much time on being cross with her—more on the thought that I was about to lose another—I can't say friend because there's no way a dog can be a real friend with cats—so let's say associate, or partner of necessity, as Joey said earlier . . . no, "partners in crime" was what That Man called the three of us once, and that was pretty groovy. But whatever she was, the thought of Joey going to her demise, let alone drowning in a storm sewer before my eyes, didn't feel very good, so I thought about what to do. Meanwhile, she was now about the width of our kitchen away from the hole, and as the water rushed her toward it fast she called out, "Goodbye, Durfy, I love you."

That struck me as really sweet, and I wished I had a rescue plan. Just as she was about to plunge down the manhole, my neck stretched out, on its own, toward her, and I took her whole head into my mouth. Then I lifted her from the water and, holding her head gently between my jaws, trotted across the street and laid her on the sidewalk. What a sight she was! I never saw any living thing, before or after that moment, as scrawny and woebegone and miserable-looking as Joey.

I was about to say to her for fun that, ironically for a cat, she was the spitting image of a drowned rat. But I couldn't, because the two workmen were making a noise with their hands and shouting. I was used to sounds like that during my nighttime rambles near neighbourhood garbage pails and homes of my dearly beloved; they were my cue to start running flat out unless I wanted to feel someone's boot or a hurled rock. Joey was sitting there licking her paws, furiously rubbing her head with them, when I said, "I don't like the sound of those guys. Let's get out of here." I took off, and Joey darted away with me as fast as she could, too.

When we stopped farther down the road, Joey said, "Thank you for saving my life, Dork. But, er, how can I say this?" She was energetically licking her paws and frantically rubbing her head, ears, and face with them again. "You need to do something about that mouth of yours. I don't know what would be worse, drowning in that filthy storm sewer or suffocating in your foul, dank dungeon of a mouth. Don't get me wrong. I appreciate your gesture. And I'm only telling you for your own good."

"I'm glad you told me, Joey. I'll put pressure on at home to get more of those mouth-freshening rawhide chews. I knew all along they weren't giving me enough. Now, since we're opening our hearts to each other about our little shortcomings, I have to tell you that, when you were heading for the manhole, you called me Durf. I'm sure you didn't mean to make that boo-boo."

"Just a near-death slip-up on my part, Dork. Won't happen again. Anything else embarrassing I should know about?"

"Well, yes. When you were saying goodbye, you said 'Durfy, I love you.'"

"Yeah, that was bad. Facing certain death must make the victim prone to deluded fantasies. The next time you lead me straight into a tragic disaster, I'll remember to keep a better grip on reality. I'll start practising for it right away." Joey whispered under her breath: "I hate you, Dork, look what you've done to me, you complete twit. I loathe you, Dork, you've gotten me killed, you total blockhead."

"Ha ha ha. Unfortunately, you'll never get a chance to use those jokes, Joey. Because as long as I'm around, something like that will never happen again."

Joey gave me her funny look. "Let's go back home, Dork," she said with a sigh. "I'm just hoping that my experience today wasn't a dress rehearsal for any worse catastrophes that might lie ahead."

That night, Joey and I became famous. Nice Woman was the first in our house to notice it. She was watching the news and suddenly said, "Look, is that Durf and Joey on TV?" It alerted the whole house, and we all rushed in and went quiet.

I heard the lady on the screen talking about a yellow Labrador retriever who had become an international hero because he'd rescued a cat that was about to drown in a flash flood. And there I was trotting along—I knew it was me, and not some other celebrity Lab, because I recognized Joey's scrawny little body hanging out of my mouth by the head. I also learned that our flight from the men working on the burst hydrant was needless, because they were actually clapping their hands and shouting, "Good dog, good dog." But how was I supposed to know that? Getting that kind of praise from human strangers was a first for me out on the mean streets of St. John's.

The workman who had videoed the scene was interviewed

on the air. He'd been getting ready to capture the flood on tape for city council, he said, when he realized that the dog was saving the cat from drowning in the storm sewer. As could be clearly seen in the video, he carefully carried the cat over to the other side of the road and gently set her down out of harm's way. I saw on the screen Joey rubbing her paws in a frenzy all over her head. I think that was when she was forming her views about the inside of my mouth. The lady on television said that news agencies around the world were vying for copies of the video and the story was going global.

"You guys are international celebrities," said That Man. And Nice Boy and Nice Girl said they couldn't wait to get to school the next morning to talk all about it to their classmates.

"Oh, this is great," Joey said to me. "Cats worldwide are going to hear that I had to be rescued by a mutt, not to mention that I actually had my head in his mouth."

"I know, right," I said. "Imagine when every dog in the universe hears that I actually saved a cat. The humiliation of the thing." We told each other that we were both too ashamed to go outside ever again.

"What were you two doing all the way over on that street?" Nice Woman asked.

"That's over a mile away," said That Man.

"I bet they were looking for Xerxes," said Nice Girl.

"Good boy, good girl," Nice Boy said, patting us. "I'm getting doggy and pussy treats for them, okay?" Nobody in the family objected, least of all Joey or me.

When I was halfway through the rawhide chew Nice Boy had given me and it was nicely covered in drool, Joey came over, looked at it, and said, "Revolting." Then she put her nose close to my lips.

"Okay, pant on me, Dork." I gave her a few quick breaths. "The chew is not working," she said, screwing up her face and walking away. "If you ever see me in water again, no more heroic measures with the mouth, okay? Just let me drown." That was a fine way for one international celebrity to talk to another! It was sad, but it looked like Joey's diva status had gone straight to her head.

Chapter 17

What Did Lassie Have That I Didn't?

The next afternoon, a man rang our doorbell and told Mrs. Rock he was a reporter who'd tracked down the identities and address of the celebrity pets through some school kids. He just needed a few snapshots.

Joey and I used the open door to skedaddle out and lope up the street. In our selfless determination to find our lost housemate, we were even willing to sacrifice the chance for more fame. Besides, the looming tragedy of Xerxes, which was my fault, was causing all this hero worship being lavished on me to lose some of its lustre.

We had only gone half a mile, in a different direction from yesterday, when we heard a voice that startled us: "Psst, Joella, Durf! Over here." Joey and I looked at each other. Xerxes? He sounded like he was outside with us. Yet I couldn't pick up his scent. We followed the sound across the street and spotted Xerxes on a windowsill looking out through a wire fly screen that was keeping the window open.

"Herpes," said Joey. "What are you doing in there?"

"This is my new home. I have a new family now."

"Your new home? What about your old home? And what are you talking about, new family? What about us? Dork and I have been searching for you for days on end to bring you back to your real home. Didn't you miss us?"

"The food is really good in this place, Joella."

"What? And I nearly drowned looking for you. Where's the gratitude here?"

"Thank you, Joella. I appreciated that. I figured you guys were looking for me. That's why I was waiting up here, just in case you went by. Because I saw on television what happened to you in the flood. You really looked brave and handsome, Durf. And Joella, you looked cute, all wet and skinny and scraggly, hanging out of Durf's mouth like something really ugly and stinky he dragged home from the dump."

"Herpes, stop making me sorry we found you. Listen. How are we going to get you out of this house?"

"There's no way out of here, Joella. They never open that front door, and the back door opens out on the backyard where they have two great big dogs running around, to prevent me from being kidnapped, my new family said. So I've moved in here for good. Well, nice seeing you guys again. Bye-bye now."

"Xerxes, you don't seem very eager to leave," I said. "You like living in this new house by the sounds of it."

"Well, besides the great food, my new bed is very soft and covered in silk, and I never find a Labrador retriever "accidentally" in it. And I don't have to share my Kitty Litter with anyone, certainly not with a cat who's not all that fussy about covering up properly. Not mentioning any names. So, all in all, it's manageable here, yes. I'm surviving." Xerxes stretched and yawned slowly and extravagantly, as if he were a cat born in Buckingham Palace. "Goodness, look, it's nap time. No need to go out of your way, guys, but do say hello if you ever happen to be in the neighbourhood again."

"Herpes, what are you saying? What about Nice Girl and Nice Boy and Nice Woman? They're worried sick about you. Don't you want to be back with them again? Even That Man misses you. He was saying only yesterday, 'Didn't we always have two cats around here? A smart one and a dim-witted one? Whatever happened to the dim-witted one?'"

I jumped in with more good arguments: "And I heard him say to Nice Woman that they had to find Xerxes, because if they were going to have cats in the house, they might as well have one that was actually a house pet, in addition to the one that always looked like it was plotting to stalk and kill a wildebeest on the African veldt."

"That Man said that? Really?" said Joey. "I always knew old Bossy Boots wasn't all bad. Anyway, Herpes, what about Nice Girl and—"

"I just knew I was forgetting something. I had this nagging feeling, but I couldn't put my finger on it. Yes, Nice Girl and Nice Boy and Nice Woman, that's it! I've got to get back to them. I really miss them now that you mention it. And That Man playing me like an accordion—how do I get out of here?"

We talked about it and thought about it, but we couldn't come up with an escape plan for Xerxes. Those two big dogs in the backyard he'd mentioned seemed to cramp our creativity. Finally, we said that Joey and I would have to go back home and tell everyone, and That Man would have to come and get him. "Xerxes," I said, "I'll have no trouble sniffing our way back here, but how come I didn't pick up your scent just then? If you hadn't called out we would have missed you completely."

"The lady here puts perfume on me," said Xerxes. "It probably masks my own scent."

"Is that the stink I'm getting?" said Joey. "Good Lord, I can't wait to rescue you from that."

"Just you hang on a minute here, Joella. That's my own special perfume, called Blue Hot Stuff. That's the kind of thing I'll be giving up if I leave here. I'm not sure you guys appreciate the sacrifices I'll be making by going back home with you."

"Oh, we do, Herpes, we do," said Joey, "don't we, Dork?"

"Oh my goodness, yes." We kept our eyes off each other so that we wouldn't burst out laughing, and we said goodbye to Xerxes for now.

On the way home, Joey said, "And Dork, just how are we going to get across to our humans where Herpes is?"

"Don't you ever watch Lassie on television, Joey?"

"Why would I watch a show about a stupid dog? Duh."

"Because they never have and never will make a show about a stupid cat, Joey. Too ridiculous and too boring to talk about."

"What about *The Cat in the Hat*?"

"Oh yeah." I had to think fast; I liked *The Cat in the Hat.* "I mean a reality show like Lassie, except about a real, live cat. How would they ever get a cat to do real-life stuff, like Lassie does? Say Lassie sees a little boy falling down an old dry well. It's too steep for him to climb out of and too deep for Lassie to reach down and pull him out of. Okay. What Lassie does is run home to the man or the woman on the show and bark to them what the situation is. Lassie will say 'ruff' and the man will ask, 'What's that you say, Lassie? Billy has fallen down an ancient well ten feet deep with steep sides?' 'Woof.'

'You say it's that well a third of a mile south-southeast of the old schoolhouse, the red one, not the new green one?' 'Wrup.' 'Take enough rope, you say, to use for climbing down and hoisting Billy back up, and some food because he's been down there for two and a half hours by now? Gotcha, Lass. Okay, gang, let's go save Billy!' See Joey? It's simple with a dog. We'll have Xerxes back in jig time."

"This I gotta see," sighed Joey.

At home, when That Man was in the living room after supper watching the news on TV, I sat down in front of him and said "Roff," meaning, "Listen up, matey. We found Xerxes; we can lead you right to him."

That Man yelled toward the door, "Durf wants to go out. I'm waiting to see an important story on the news. Somebody please let Durf out."

I went up closer to him and said, "Yerp," meaning, "It's not far away. I know the exact house. Come on, let's go." And I walked to the door and looked back at him.

"Somebody, anybody, please! I'm right in the middle of the news. Durf needs to go out."

Nice Woman called back, "I'm on a long-distance phone call."

Nice Girl said, "I've got to go. Sandra and her mother are out there waiting for me in the car."

Nice Boy said, "Durf doesn't need to go out. I just let him in."

I came back and said to That Man, "Wurf, riff," meaning, "Xerxes is right up in the window where you can see him. You can't miss him. Come on, stop dragging your heels, dude, we've got to go. Now!"

"Durf, will you stop bugging me." That Man got up, took hold of my collar, led me out into the hall, went back in the living room, and closed the door behind him.

Joey was sitting in the hall licking her paws and washing her face. She briefly opened her eyes to look at me. "If I were you, Dorky," she said, "I wouldn't bother trying out for the Lassie role."

"The mistake I made was thinking That Man was smart like the guy in Lassie. We're going to have to rescue Xerxes ourselves the next time we sneak out. You with me on that?"

"Oh yes, I'm with you. What's our plan for breaking the prisoner out without getting killed ourselves?"

"We'll think of one, Joey. Have I ever let you down yet?"

Joey mustn't have heard me, because she didn't answer. Instead, she lay down on the floor and put her paws on top of her head.

Chapter 18

Hercules Comes Home

We were able to sneak out of the house while the kids were helping their dad bring in a much-talked-about air purifier from the car. "What do you figure that thing is for?" I wondered to Joey.

"You," said Joey.

"You're too kind," I said. "When we get Xerxes back, I'm sure he'll want you to share the credit."

"Oh, I'm sure he'll be all high and mighty about the Kitty Litter again. Really! I sometimes wonder why I'm even doing this."

Quickly, we made our way to the house where Xerxes was being held hostage. There he was, up on his window sill looking out through the screen, waiting for us. "Where's That Man?" he asked. "I thought you were going to bring him here to rescue me."

"We told him the kidnappers were demanding a ransom of one dollar," said Joey. "He was so shocked by the amount, he had to sit down."

"It does sound like a lot," said Xerxes.

"I'll say. It's nearly as much as a can of cat food costs. 'What?'

he said, 'I don't know about this—a dollar for a matted-haired, bluish, cat-like thingamajig who can't tell a mouse from a giraffe?'"

"That's not my fault. It wasn't part of my mother's training. She spent her time showing me how to sit on a velvet cushion looking majestic. So you're saying I'm finished, then. It's all over for me. I stay here forever."

"Sure looks like it, Herpy. Would you mind that?"

"Well . . . you mentioned the can of cat food. I really miss that. All I get here is salmon and steak and old stuff. And I was thinking all about Nice Girl and Nice Boy and Nice Woman and That Man while I was waiting for you. I thought you said they really wanted me back. What went wrong, I wonder?"

I couldn't stand his heartbroken sound. "Xerks, Joey doesn't seem to know when it's not appropriate to tease someone," I said. "Everybody, That Man included, wants you back. Joey was only joking."

"I knew that," said Xerxes, perking right up.

"I was trying to keep from you the real reason That Man is not here," said Joey. "It's because Dork was trying to be like Lassie on TV and That Man was trying to understand him like the guy in the show, but instead they were like Abbott and Costello in 'Who's on First.'"

"Yeah, something got lost in the translation, Xerks," I said. "So we've got to do this ourselves." I noticed that the backyard gate was open. "Where are those big dogs you mentioned gone?"

"I saw them going out for a walk with their man here. He had them on their leashes, so everything should be fine."

"Okay, how are we going to get you out?" As we talked and tried to figure out the escape plan, none of us noticed that the resident dogs and their man had just come over the hill. When I smelled something dangerous on the wind and looked around, I saw the dogs glaring down at Joey and me standing on their lawn. They lunged, yanking the leashes out of their master's hand, and came tearing down the hill toward us.

"Joey, run away and hide," I said. "Climb a tree or a pole or something."

"What about you, Dork? Will they hurt you?"

"I can take care of myself," I said, acting the big hero, forgetting for the moment that there were two of them and only one of me. Math was never my strong subject.

Suddenly they were close. Those mastiffs could move. They were defending their own territory, which increased their strength and desire to attack. They weren't making a sound but their hackles were up, and their canine teeth showed in a blood-curdling way. Then they growled low, encouraging each other to massacre me. Before I knew it, the two of them were on top of me.

One seized the loose skin around my neck in his jaws and, snarling fiercely, inched his teeth closer and closer to my throat. The other sank his teeth into my haunch and pulled me down on my back on the ground. I could hear their man shouting commands at them from a distance, but they were crazy with rage and paid no attention. They stayed focused on killing me.

I was about to give up, and hoped to survive by going into submissive mode, when I saw out of the corner of my eye a missile flying through the air toward us. It struck the dog that was working on my neck right in the side of the head. Then, instead of dropping to the ground, the projectile stayed on the dog's face. It turned out to be Joey.

Her front claws were sunk into the dog's snout, and she was biting his nose desperately, and kicking his ear repeatedly with her hind paws. The dog let out a yelp and let go of my throat. This allowed me to seize the other dog by the neck in my jaws and tear him loose from my haunch. He managed to free himself from my jaws with more strength than I'd ever felt in another dog, and for a few seconds we were in a standoff as he readied himself to attack again.

I saw the other dog bash Joey against the wall next to Xerxes's window and then fling her loose from his head. She struck the wall again, hard, before dropping down behind a low bush. I could see her tail. She was not scurrying away, or even moving. The dog moved toward the bush and I turned to try to stop him. If he reached Joey, that would be the end of her. But the other dog leaped on top of me from behind and seized me by the neck.

Then I heard Xerxes behind the screen yowling and caterwauling—something I'd never known him to do before. The noise caught the attention of the dog near Joey, and he turned with a vicious growl to attack Xerxes, the more obvious victim. Furiously, the dog rammed into the screen, snout first. The screen and Xerxes flew back into the room and landed on the floor. The window, without the screen to hold it up, came down on the dog's neck. It trapped him there, with his body outside and his head inside, snarling and yelping. He frantically tried to pull his head out from under the window but couldn't.

By now the dogs' human had arrived. He grabbed the leash of the dog on top of me and pulled him off, and, for good measure, kicked me in the ribs. I don't know what some guys seem to have against my ribs. I ran over to find Joey. She was still there behind the bush, lying on her side on the ground. She looked up at me as I nosed her: "I'm okay, I'm okay," she said, "Just winded. Is there any way we can get Herpes out?"

I bawled out to Xerxes to jump up to the window and squeeze out through the space under it. I never saw Xerxes move so fast. He leaped up on the sill again and, staying as far as he could from the snarling dog's teeth, thrust his head into the gap. I was afraid he mightn't be able to cram the rest of his body through, but it was amazing how much of his bulk disappeared into flattened fur as he scrambled under the window and jumped down on the lawn.

The man shouted, "Hercules, come back."

"Hercules: that's my new name," said Xerxes, scrambling away from him and the dog straining at the leash.

"Named after another brilliant loser," said Joey, hobbling along.

"Gee whiz, was Hercules a loser, too?" said Xerxes. "No wonder I'm a bundle of complexes."

"He started out okay—if a bit dumb," said Joey, "but he ended badly."

"Guys, listen," I said, "can you talk about all that on the therapy couch later? Right now we've got to make tracks."

The man had all he could do to control the dog he was holding on the leash as he went to the other dog, grabbed his leash, too, in the same hand, and pushed the window up to release him. Any second I expected one of the dogs, or both, to burst loose and chase us down. Xerxes and Joey wouldn't stand a chance. The man yelled at us, "It's no use running away. We'll catch up with you."

Xerxes couldn't move very fast and wouldn't last long running anyway, so I said to him, "Hop up on my back, Xerks." He knew exactly what to do, because we'd often played games around the house for the kids, with the cats riding on my back, falling off, and jumping up again, having fun. Once up there today, though, Xerxes clung on tight for dear life, all his claws digging through the fur far deeper than usual into my skin. I could feel him quivering, and I didn't have the heart to tell him to loosen up a bit on the death-grip before he skinned me alive.

Meanwhile, Joey was trying to trot normally along beside me, but she was lagging behind and I could see that she was injured and in pain. For starters, her tail had a kink in it worse than mine. I told her to jump up on my back and hang on, too. She made a couple of offers to spring up, but when she didn't do it, I knew she couldn't. I stopped and got down on my stomach, and she dragged herself up on my back. Once they were both safely there, I took off down the sidewalk fast, heading for home.

Behind us we could hear the man with the dogs shouting, "I'll find you. I know where you live."

"That guy is a hit man," said Joey. "I'll never call That Man a member of the Mafia again. Compared to buddy with the mutts back there, he's Florence Nightingale."

Xerxes said, "Well, I know where that dog guy lives, too; he's not the only one who can play this hit-man game."

"Good to have you back, Herp," said Joey. "I feel safer already."

On the way home, a lot of pedestrians and people in cars slowed down to look at me and the two cats on my back. Some even took pictures. "Oh no," I shouted over my shoulder to Joey and Xerxes, "don't tell me this is going to be on television, too. It'll kill me with all my true loves when they see me carrying a load of cats through town on my back."

"Well, I'm all right with being on television," said Xerxes. "I missed out on the superstar status you two got from the dramatic flood rescue."

"Yes, that was a shame, Herpes," said Joey. "But tell you what. You can have the glamorous movie role they offered me to play a half-drowned rat being carried by the head out of a sewer by a junkyard dog."

"Let me sleep on that, Joella."

When we got home, none of the family was in the house and it was Mrs. Rock's day off. Meanwhile, Joey was whimpering a little to herself when she thought we couldn't hear, and I was bleeding from my neck and at the top of a hind leg. But we'd have to wait for help until someone in our family arrived.

As we lay there close to the door, I got a chance to thank Joey for helping me when I was under attack from both dogs. "Where did you get the idea of flying through the air like a cannonball and striking the dog in the head like that? From your mother at the barn?"

"Partly, but I saw it on television, too," said Joey. "They showed a video of a cat doing it to save a boy who was being attacked by a dog."

"I saw that video, too," said Xerxes. "If they ever decide to make a series about it, I'm going to audition for it. Unless you want the role, Joella. But you're probably sick and tired of being a celebrity by now."

We passed our time like that, analyzing the ups and downs of being famous, and dealing with Xerxes's questions on the pros and cons of our celebrity status. Suddenly I smelled those vicious dogs.

I confess that, after our savage ruckus with them, my first impulse was to run away from here as fast as I could and save myself. But I resisted that urge, and instead I moved toward the scent. This might well be my last day on earth, but I was determined to defend those under my protection, Joey and Xerxes. Looking around me, though, I saw no dogs. Their man shut the door of the car he'd just gotten out of and started to walk down the driveway toward us. The smell of the dogs was coming off him.

"Hello, Hercules," he said, looking at Xerxes. "I've come to save you from the clutches of these two pirates. But first I have to see if there's anyone home." He pressed the doorbell button by the side door and waited. When no one came out, he said, "Good, no complications," and walked toward us. "Now I'll just gather you up, my kitty, and we'll be on our way home for that lovely snack of sardines waiting for you there. Samantha told me not to come home without the world's most handsome pussy."

"Hear that?" said Xerxes. "Samantha is some nice. She's the woman of the house. Well, great seeing you guys." He walked toward the man.

"What are you doing, Herpes?" said Joey. "We nearly got killed getting way from there. You don't want to go back now, do you?"

"What? Oh. No, no, I don't. He had me mesmerized there for a minute with all his sweet talk. No, I want to stay here with you guys and my real family."

"Okay then, get behind us," I said. "You're not going anywhere you don't want to go."

"Out of the way, you hell-hound," said the man, "unless you want another kick in the ribs. And you, you scrawny alley cat, you buzz off, too, or I'll show Wolf where you live. He'll be glad to have the information so he can even the score for those scratches you put on his face."

I didn't know about Joey, but that did it for me. I started to bark and growl ferociously and raised my hackles. And the foot he threatened me with, I made for, and grabbed his ankle in my jaws, pressing hard enough to show I meant business—not enough to break the skin beneath his pant leg and sock, not intentionally anyway, but hey, who was going to be that particular in my situation? He yelled in pain and swore and tried to shake me loose from his leg, grabbing my collar to pull me off.

Meanwhile, Joey, despite her injuries, rose to the challenge, too. She limped as fast as she could over to his other ankle and dug in, teeth and claws. He finally managed to shake and pull us off, but only because we let go. He backed away and turned and trotted to his car, with Joey's snarl following him: "Now you go on home and compare your scratches with the ones I gave your precious Wolf."

"You guys are a darn good team," said Xerxes. "Normally I don't condone violence, but when the cause is good, then it's acceptable."

"Like when we're rescuing your beautiful hide, you mean?" said Joey.

"Yes," said Xerxes, "that sort of thing."

Chapter 19

Xerxes is Forced to Curb His Wild Streak

When my family got home in the late afternoon, they found the three of us lying on the lawn, snuggled together for comfort and security. Nice Girl and Nice Boy were ecstatic to see Xerxes, of course, and Joey and I could understand it if they took turns cuddling him more than us, just this once. But everyone's happiness was short-lived when they saw that Joey was limping and that there was dried blood on my neck and hind leg, Moreover, Joey's tail, and not mine for a change, became a focus of curiosity. Nice Woman went right in and made an appointment with the veterinarian, and That Man drove us all out to see her right away.

When we went into her clinic, the vet was so glad to see me she singled me out in her greeting: "Oh, look, surprise! Durf is here again." And she gave me a friendly pat of welcome on the head.

As she examined the three of us, she asked, "Anyone know what happened here?"

That Man explained that Xerxes had gone missing for days

and then he'd shown up with us on the doorstep, today, out of nowhere.

"Well, Xerxes is in good shape," she said. "He seems well-fed and has no injuries and isn't sick and is well-groomed. Someone was taking care of him, for sure. But these other two scallywags look like they came through the wars."

I had a bruised rib, which might be cracked, and some dog bites which she cleaned up and gave me a needle for. Joey was in no better shape. She had a sprained hind leg which would make her hobble three-legged for a while, and a broken tail which, the vet said, would keep her from sailing through the air like a flying squirrel for a time. She put the tail in a splint and said she thought she could save it but, even if she didn't have to amputate, it might have a twist in it from now on. "With their tails so similar," she said, "Durf and Joey are going to be mistaken for the Bobbsey Twins." It made the humans laugh, but Joey scowled and said that she failed to see the humour.

"I'm flattered, though, Joey," I said. "I had no idea you wanted to copy my tail so badly."

"If it does turn out like yours, Dork, I'll have it amputated, don't worry."

"Oh, don't do that, Joella," said Xerxes. "I think it's really cute that my two favourite subjects both ended up with silly-looking tails."

"Herpy," said Joey. "I know we're giddy with survivor's euphoria, and that it gives us a feeling that we are close comrades who will tolerate anything from each other, but don't push me, okay?"

"Sorry, Joella, my bad. It's just that I'm so happy."

"Yes, I know. You're happy because we're all together again, but settle down now and be your normal namby-pamby self, just the way everyone likes you."

"No, I'm happy because I haven't got a scratch on me, even though you guys got roughed up real bad."

Joey had to laugh. I think it was the first time I'd ever seen her actually laugh. "Well, *I'm* glad we're all together again, Herps. And thank you for saving my life with your caterwauling when the dog was about to eat me. You sounded really good, just like a real cat."

"Thank you, Joella. I'm glad it worked, but I did feel a bit awkward doing it. I hope I'm never called upon to do it again. Because you're right. I need to settle down and conduct myself with majestic dignity again. Even today, I was starting to feel a little out of place, making sizzling conversation."

When we all got home again, the family tried to figure out what had happened to Joey and me, and how come Xerxes was suddenly back unscathed, with no signs of wear and tear. They couldn't fathom any of it. Then, abruptly, I sniffed that vicious dog scent again, just before the doorbell rang. I kept myself back, hovering between alarm and hostility. One of the kids answered the door and called out, "Dad, there's a man here to see you."

As That Man went out, I trotted behind him. The sight of the familiar dog man standing at the door made me bark and growl and strut about, hackles up. I couldn't help myself. That Man stopped and turned around to me. "What's going on, Durf? Stop that." Then he said to the man, "I don't know what's gotten into him. He's never like that when anyone comes to the door. Can I help you?"

"Is your dog safe?" asked the man at the door, stepping back a couple of steps, "Or is he out of control again?"

"Again?" said That Man. "When was he out of—"

Joey had arrived at the door, and now she started up. She arched her back and hobbled sideways, meowing loudly, almost screeching, and then she flattened herself to the hall floor, laid her ears tightly back on her head, flicked her splinted tail back and forth, and hissed ferociously. "You too, Joey? What's the matter with you guys?"

The other man said, "I have a couple of dogs at home. Maybe they're smelling them off me and it's getting their dander up. I won't keep you long. I have reason to believe that a cat of ours, a blue Persian by the name of Hercules, is in this house."

"A Persian cat called Hercules? Here? Why on earth would you have reason to believe that?"

"I was here this afternoon and saw him with your vicious dog and cat in your driveway. Hercules escaped from our house earlier and must have followed them here."

"We do have a blue Persian here, Xerxes, who went missing a week or so ago, and then came back this afternoon. He's in too good a shape to have been wandering around outside all that time, so we suspect someone kidnapped him from our property, and brought him to their house."

"Well, the best of luck in finding your cat. Would you be good enough to hand over our cat? My wife sent me to get him; she's absolutely heartbroken that he's gone."

"Before I hand him over, I need to make sure he's yours. Does he have a registration number?"

"Gosh, I don't know. My wife got him from someone. Does yours have a number?"

"Yes."

"And what would the number be? I can check it with my wife."

"You tell me. Oh, I know what you can do. Come in the house

right now and phone your wife and ask her for the registration number on Hercules's certificate."

"She's not home now. I'll check with her and get back to you. Meanwhile, if you don't give him up peacefully, I'll have no option but to inform the police of the theft of our valuable property."

"Yes, you do that. What's your name and address in case we ever need to touch base with you—if our Xerxes goes missing again, for instance?"

"Your lawyer can get that information from the police."

That Man followed the other guy out the walk and went to the rear of his vehicle. There he wrote in his notebook. "Okay, I have your licence number. That'll get me all the info I need, including how our dog and our other cat got so banged up when they were bringing our Persian back home. I'm thinking it was because they were looking out for Xerxes. They're all great buddies. This whole mystery is starting to unravel."

The other man didn't answer, and got in his car. But Joey said: "Herpes and me great buddies! What a whopper!" She looked around to make sure Xerxes heard her teasing remark. But he had disappeared. "Hey, where's he gone?"

Joey and I found Xerxes hiding in the back of a dark closet upstairs. "Has he left?" he asked.

"Yes," said Joey, "and I don't think he'll be back, judging by the fear in his eyes when he was looking at me."

"Thanks, Joella. I wouldn't go near him because I was afraid he might sweet-talk me into going back with him again. Oh, it was very stylish and sophisticated there and all that, and I was finally treated like a proper king, but I'd rather give up that royal life and make this personal sacrifice by staying here for the benefit of my own humble subjects."

"Would your majesty happen to be including me among your majesty's humble subjects, by any chance," asked Joey, advancing on Xerxes.

"Oh my goodness, no!" said Xerxes. "I was thinking more along the lines of Durf and That Man." At that instant, we heard from downstairs the tune that That Man always whistled to induce Xerxes to come to him and be played like an accordion.

"That's one of my subjects now," said Xerxes, ambling fast toward the staircase. "Hold that thought, Joella. You have my permission to approach me with it later." Joey and I trotted after him to make sure he wasn't about to receive anything that we might want, too.

Down in the kitchen, That Man picked up Xerxes and stretched and compressed him a half-dozen times, accompanied by deafening purring. Then he sat down and placed Xerxes, squirming under protest at being de-accordioned, on his lap, and parted the thicket of hair in one of his ears. "Yes, here it is," he said, peering at something. "It's really hard to see, but the number is tattooed right there that proves you're our very own registered purebred aristocratic feline, straight from the shelter." He compared the number to the one on a piece of paper he picked up from the table.

"See, I told you," said Xerxes to us as we watched. "I hope you guys are ashamed of yourselves now for disrespecting me."

"Herpes, the vet put that number there to show that you had your operation," said Joey. "Sure, I've got one of those, and how purebred do you figure I am?"

"Expressed like that, you do have a good point, Joella. But Durf has one in his ear, too—I've seen it—and he's not improved, remember? His is there to prove how exclusive he is, just like mine."

I couldn't let Joey feel bad that she was being left out of having a tattoo proving she was a top-notch pet, not after the way she saved me in that fight with the dog, so I said, "Yeah, but I got mine before this kink in my tail showed up and put me out of the running. So, it's meaningless, might as well not be there at all. I'm happy just being a regular guy."

"It's easy to act like you're just a regular guy, Durf," Xerxes said, "when you're a big international celebrity hero, like you. But what about someone relatively unknown like me? Now this is going to sound silly, I know, but sometimes I almost think that maybe I don't deserve my high position in life. It's almost as if I'm not entitled to this elite status. I'm starting to think I should pretend I'm just commonplace and run-of-the-mill like you, Joella. I'm going to start practising right away being equal. Comrade Joella—how does that sound? This is going to be hard to believe, but I fantasized up there in that closet earlier that from now on I'm going to be ordinary, just very, very ordinary like you. What do you think of that idea, comrade?"

"You fantasized about being very, very ordinary, did you, Herpes? Well, it's always nice when your fantasy and your reality turn out to be identical."

"I'm glad you agree, Comrade Joella. It's important to me to have my former subjects on side. Comrade Durf, what's your viewpoint? Don't be intimidated by my past high status. You don't have to honey-coat your opinion. I'm not impressed by a yes-man. I'm giving you permission to speak freely."

"Whatever you do," said Joey, "don't give your former subject, That Man, permission to speak freely. We'll all need earplugs."

That made me laugh, but kind-heartedly and without malice, because, of course, I loved and respected That Man dearly.

"I don't see any humour in me lowering myself to the level of you guys," said Xerxes. "I see only indignity, but I'm willing—" I heard the phone ringing, and ran out to listen. Xerxes said, "Comrade Durf! I don't recall dismissing you."

I had to pay close attention to phone conversations, because I never knew when someone was going to deliver fresh rainbow trout afterwards. A couple of years ago, when the phone rang one time, I foolishly did not listen carefully to what That Man said, and it was followed by the delivery a short while later of some rainbow trout by his brother. But not knowing that, I snuck through the door as he was coming in and nearly missed out completely. I only got one tiny, maddeningly delicious sample, because Mrs. Rock saved it for me, and, meanwhile, the cats tortured me with descriptions of the big filets they said they received. A trout delivery could happen again any time that phone rang, and no way was I going to be robbed of my rightful share this time.

That Man picked up the phone now, said hello, and listened for a while. Then he said, "If you or your husband come around our house to kidnap Xerxes again, we'll be calling the police. We have your name and address. Consider yourself warned." And he banged down the receiver. Yet another phone conversation without a single darn word about trout.

That Man told Nice Woman that the woman on the phone had claimed that Xerxes—she called him Hercules—was hers. "Imagine," he said, "calling a Persian cat by a Greco-Roman name." Say what you will about That Man, he certainly knew a lot of useless old stuff to argue about. He continued, "The woman said that she and her husband found him abandoned and lost on the street with no human assistance around, but with two large dogs in the vicinity that could easily have mauled him. She claims she saved Hercules's life that day and spared him a lifetime of neglect and abuse from us, his supposed caregivers. She says she's going to keep an eye on our property to record it on camera the next time he's abandoned and left in mortal danger, and she says she's going to report us to the authorities. She can only make an educated guess about our parenting, she says. But, since we so badly neglected Hercules and are known to have produced another savage cat and vicious dog, she shudders at how terribly neglected and abused our own children must be."

"What?" said Nice Woman, abruptly jumping up. "That is the last straw." I'd never seen her look so angry before.

"I know," said That Man. "Those two psychos are dangerous."

The same day, I heard him and Nice Woman on the phone instructing their lawyer to notify the police by letter, detailing the events to date, with a copy by registered mail to, as Joey had named them, "the Two Crazies."

That was not the last we heard of the man or his wife. We saw them on the television news a few weeks later when he was charged with offenses under the Dog Act. His two dogs had escaped from his backyard and attacked a small dog and its woman who were walking by their house. Both "suffered serious but non-life-threatening injuries" before the guy was able to pull them off. He ended up being fined a small amount and was required to sign an undertaking to henceforth keep his two dogs under proper care and control.

Our humans were now able to make the connection between the man's dogs and the injuries Joey and I had suffered. But unfortunately they couldn't prove it. Nice Boy and Nice Girl said to us it wasn't fair that the courts wouldn't accept evidence from me and the cats so that the perp could receive a more serious punishment for what had happened to us.

Then we learned that, as a result of the letter our humans had sent to the police, plus other questionable activities as reported by a neighbour, an officer investigated further and discovered that the woman was keeping more than twenty cats in a room in their house. Because of the conditions, they had to be distributed to legitimate, properly run animal shelters.

The woman went on television to complain. She explained the presence of all the animals as her "cat rescue operation." When she first saved a cat, she would care for it in a room by itself until it was brought back to good health before she placed it in the rescue room with all the others. And then she'd rush right out and save another one. Her operation might not be one hundred per cent perfect in terms of space, food, and Kitty Litter, but any civilized and compassionate person must agree, she stated confidently on TV, that the care and food they received were far better than the fate suffered by homeless, starving cats on the street, or cats doomed to suffer appallingly in homes of abusive owners.

"Which were you, Xerxes . . . starving, homeless, or abused?" asked That Man. Xerxes jumped up on his lap and pushed at his hands, until he held him and played him like an accordion. "And that poor woman. You hardly know whether she's to be pitied, blamed, or admired."

"Well, I certainly know!" said Nice Woman without elaborating, leaving us hanging. She picked up Joey and scratched her ears.

Nice Boy and Nice Girl, who were sitting on the sofa with their feet on my back, giving it a good rub as I lay on the floor, laughed in appreciation of their mother's reaction. "We can do up an affidavit, if you want, Mom," said Nice Girl, "saying that you didn't neglect and abuse us too, too badly."

"Speak for yourself," said Nice Boy.

"Very funny," said Nice Woman. "But remember, it's not too late for the abuse to start."

During the next few days, reaction to the woman's "cat rescue operation" divided into two opposing views on call-in shows and in letters to the editor. Some people declared that the woman deserved the Order of Canada, if not a Nobel Peace Prize for her good intentions, and others claimed that she should be investigated by Amnesty International for crimes against animals for operating an underground "cat dungeon."

Two callers stated that they had found, among the woman's "rescued" cats, their own cats that had gone missing without explanation months ago. One of the callers thanked the woman for preserving their cat from harm all these months. The other alleged flatly that their cat, which had played for a year around their house without incident, was kidnapped.

"All I know," Joey said, "is that another day or two there in that house, Herpy, and we could kiss your escape goodbye. You would have been dumped by then in the rescue room with all the other saved cats."

"I can't thank you guys enough for your support and assistance," said Xerxes. "It must be good sometimes to be like you, Joella—so homely and savage that no one would even bother to rescue you like they did to me."

"Oh, you're welcome, Herp," said Joey, shaking her head.

But Xerxes's envy was sincere. In the aftermath of his kidnapping and escape, he continued that line of thought. He complained that the ordeal had deprived him of an exciting life. Just before all that happened, he said, he had been well on his way to a wild and merry career in the streets and back alleys just like the life Joella enjoyed. But now he was going to have to cold-bloodedly nip in the bud that untamed and rowdy streak he'd been delighted to discover in his character, not because of the danger to himself, but so as to protect his family from further heartbreak and accusations: "I can never leave the house again; it's the only way for my loved ones to avoid any more confrontations with catjackers."

"Don't worry, nobody's ever going to do that again," said Joey, displaying her claws and teeth. "And Dork, show him that horrendous mouth of choppers you've got. See, Herpes? No need to fret. "

Every time Joey and I got ready to sneak out through a door left open a few seconds too long, she'd whisper, "Come on, Herps, let's go."

I don't know what I would have done if Xerxes had started to head out, but he only murmured, from atop his favourite overstuffed easy chair, "See you guys later, have fun," and turned over, with a languorous stretch and yawn.

Chapter 20

The Rescue I Couldn't Make

The years of family togetherness in our house flew by. Xerxes and Joey seemed happy enough, but I faked my contentment a lot so as not to hurt the feelings of my humans. They were doing their best, but the situation was out of their control, and I hid from them my frustration at the way I was forced to live. Joey put her toe right on the problem, though. "Dork," she said, "so far you've saved a little girl and her mother from a rampaging bull moose, and you rescued a hare-brained teenager from freezing to death in the snow, and—"

"Don't forget how he rescued me from that kidnapper and his killer dogs and the dungeon of doom," said Xerxes.

Joey looked daggers at him and stood up: "Herp, I was there, too."

"Yes, I know, I know, Joella, you helped, too. No need to come over and beat the face off me."

"Maybe later," said Joey. "So, Dorky, you've made at least three heroic rescues to date, all land-based. Not one of them involved those webbed toes of yours. Now, I ask you, am I the only one who sees the irony here? In spite of the fact that you are a water dog, none of your daring rescues have been in water. Even when you so graciously yanked me by the head out of the flooded gutter, you were standing on terra firma and only used your mouth. Your webbed toes didn't come into play at all."

"Aren't you forgetting the time I saved That Man in the swimming pool?" I asked. "I used my webbed toes that day, big time."

"Er, Dork, I was going to pass over that episode in silence. I heard through the grapevine it didn't end all that well."

"Well, if it didn't, why didn't it?" I said. "Purely because the survivor would not co-operate and stubbornly saved himself to keep me from getting the glory."

"Precisely. Hence, what are we left with? This utter travesty: in spite of all your land-based rescues thus far, the human busybodies in this town have gone ahead and enforced a law preventing you and your fellow mongrels and mutts from venturing out the door by yourself onto that very land. You are never again allowed out in public without being on a leash and accompanied by a human. Taboo. Absolutely verboten. And just how, may I ask, are you supposed to perform any more of your courageous land rescues in days to come? Does anyone else but me see something self-defeating and ironic with this picture?"

"And to rub Durf's nose in it," said Xerxes, "That Man has credited him with single-handedly bringing in the strict enforcement of the law. He says that it was Durf running amok out on the streets over the years that has forced the powers that be to stop dog owners from letting their dogs roam around loose. He says that Durf and his berserk rampages throughout the city ended up performing a tremendous service for the human citizens."

"Yeah," I said, "That Man says that the epitaph on my headstone should read, 'Here lies our beloved Durf: Hoist with his own petard.' Whatever that meant. But it must be bad, because everything has certainly changed for the worse out there. You never see a dog roving aimlessly about the streets anymore now, not like in the good old days. It's pitiful. The last time I managed to sneak out—when Granny came to visit last week—it was like a nuclear winter out there. Not a dog, not even a crackie in sight anywhere."

"Well, thank heavens Granny can't stand you," said Joey, "or you wouldn't have had even that much freedom. She left that back door open on purpose. Did you hear what she said when you took off out of the house? 'Goodbye, Durf. No need to come back.'"

"She said, 'No need to *hurry* back.' Enjoy myself out there, in other words. You shouldn't badmouth our senior citizens like that, Joey. Everyone knows she loves me to pieces."

"While everyone is busy loving everyone else all to pieces," said Xerxes, "what about me? No one has come to grips with the really important question here. If it's a crime for dogs to be out by themselves these days, how is Durf supposed to rescue me the next time I get kidnapped? Am I alone in seeing the huge potential for tragic overtones here?"

"But Herpes," said Joey, "we can't have Dork out there saving you if there's a risk some citizen might be a little bit offended by the sight of him."

"Joella, whose side are you on, anyway?"

"Yours, Herpes. I was just being sarcastic."

"Oh, okay. I love it when you're sarcastic."

"I'm surprised that a cat of your intellect likes sarcasm, Herp, since sarcasm is the lowest form of wit."

"Help me out here, Durf," said Xerxes. "Was she being sarcastic again, then? I can never tell if Joella is complimenting me or insulting me. She is kinda cute, though."

There had been a time when, if Xerxes applied the word "cute" to Joey, it would have brought a tap from the paw of the little barn cat. But she had gradually stopped doing that almost entirely. She could still be as saucy as ever sometimes, but the years seemed to have mellowed her, and I noticed that she and I were agreeing on things more and more. Or maybe it was me who was mellowing. I didn't have the heart to tell her that, although I didn't see any dogs when I was last outside, I did see a big oversupply of pesky cats on the loose; they had the run of the darn town. In years gone by, I would have organized a demonstration of kinky-tailed canines to protest and give chase, but I was valuing my comfortable companionship with Joey too much these days to create a civil war over it. I even suppressed my jealousy over her being able to sneak outside every couple of days.

Xerxes had just said he was worried about the potential for tragic overtones involving himself. But I was to discover that tragedy can strike unexpectedly out of the blue and in ways you never imagined possible. What broke my heart, on top of the grief that struck us, was that unlike in the past, I wasn't there to prevent it.

Nice Boy and Nice Girl had passed through high school and were young adults now. Most of the time, these days, they were either away at university, or working, or travelling. Because Nice Woman and That Man were sometimes absent, too, on business or holiday, plans had to be made to look after the needs of us "three amigos." Often, a relative or friend came in and minded the house. Now and then, arrangements would be made for Xerxes, Joey, and me to grace the homes of friends of the family eager to have our fascinating company for a few days.

Then came an occasion when the three of us had to be divided up. Xerxes went to the home of Nice Girl's friend; one pussycat was as much as the friend could manage for two weeks, she said, and I didn't blame her because Joey was still a handful. So, a friend of Nice Woman's, who'd always liked Joey's style, was delighted to have her stay with her in her house outside St. John's. She wanted me to come, too. She and her husband were thinking of getting a Lab of their own and needed to see if they had what it took to be worthy friends with a canine of my stature.

Joey asked me to go with her, and normally I would've been eager to join them. But That Man happened to mention the boarding kennel I'd stayed at before, hosted by a kind man and woman renowned for their stock of treats and chews. The idea of a holiday there, spending positive time again describing the riveting story of my life to the spellbound assembly of other dogs, was too appealing to resist. I jumped around at the mention of the kennel, and that's where I went. Fate can be so fickle and cruel.

The friend who took Joey told us afterwards that the beautiful little cat would sit on the back of her sofa and look out the front window all the time trying to spot wildlife in the big field across the road. If she saw a field mouse or a vole or a shrew, she would start chittering and run to the door, wanting to go outside and begin the hunt. Nice Woman and That Man had told their friend that Joey was used to being outside and there was no need to be too worried about her getting out. But the friend was reluctant because a couple of big dogs roamed the area, and Joey, being a townie cat, mightn't be savvy enough to avoid them. It never occurred to the friend that the country road, which carried hardly any traffic when compared with the city streets that Joey was used to, would present a serious danger.

On the last day of her visit with the friend, Joey crept up to the door and, while her host was paying the paper boy, slipped outside. The woman ran out after her and saw her on the shoulder, stalking something she was focused on in the field. Then Joey charged across the road toward her prey just as a pickup truck, heading for the wharf, came careening down toward her. Before the friend's horrified eyes, Joey was struck by a big front tire. The friend and her husband rushed her to a vet who said that she had died instantly: everyone could take solace from the fact that she hadn't suffered at all.

But we suffered. It was impossible for anyone in my house to believe that such an accident could take our clever, street-smart, wild-but-careful Joey. The poor friend broke into tears a dozen times, blaming herself, as she described what had happened. Nice Woman and That Man told her that it wasn't her fault: you couldn't keep Joey in if she was determined to go out. And she had died happy, doing what she loved; she was simply too much of a warrior and hunter to be controlled. It was a miracle that something like this hadn't happened before.

My two grown-ups tried to be brave, but I could see how sad they were as they went silently about the house. And it nearly killed them to have to telephone Nice Girl and Nice Boy and tell them of the tragedy. The kids were devastated; their first thought was that they had to fly home right away for a proper funeral. But their parents convinced them that they would attend to the burial themselves for now, with an appropriate memorial ceremony in the backyard the next time the whole family was home together.

I was heartbroken and guilt-ridden. If I hadn't been so intent on playing the big hero again at the kennel—if only I'd gone with Joey instead—I was sure the tragedy wouldn't have happened. I would have been there to protect her. I didn't know how, but I knew I would have kept her safe. I don't believe I would ever have recovered from my grief and remorse if Xerxes had not been affected by Joey's death even more than me. I had to forget about myself and look after him.

But despite everything I did—the nuzzles, licks, naps between my paws, rides on my back—it was Xerxes who never recovered.

He kept moving about the house, looking under beds and into dark closets, expecting to find her somewhere. When he lay between my front paws, he would always nudge the space next to him with his own paw as he was waking up, expecting to touch Joey. But then when he'd open his eyes and see that she wasn't there, he would let out a low, mournful meow. As time went on, Xerxes's mind was affected by Joey's absence ever more.

He couldn't be bothered with his food and wouldn't go to his bowl to eat. It could stay there untouched all day, for all he cared. Even when someone carried him there, or brought food to him, he only picked at it "to keep everybody happy," he'd say to me, and before long he stopped nibbling altogether.

Over time, whenever I tried to interest Xerxes in life again— it shouldn't have been that hard, since there was nothing very complicated to his life—he looked at me and listened politely, until he couldn't even make-believe he cared anymore. As he faded, he started asking me, "If it's not too much trouble, Durf, would you mind calling me Herpes sometimes?" After I'd done that once or twice, he began to ask, "Durf, would it be all right if I called you 'Dorky' now and then?"

"Any time you feel like it, Herpes."

"Okay, and can you give me a little tap on the cheek with your paw like Joella did when I said something she pretended she didn't like?"

"But she gave that up when she got older and more sensible, didn't she?"

"Yes, and I didn't like it one bit. Whenever she used to do it before, I knew she was really there for me."

"Well, I don't want to hurt you with my big paw, Herpy."

"Just a little tap, Dork. Joella never hurt when she did it. She never had her claws out, even with you."

Xerxes's memory was rather favourably selective if that was how he remembered Joey's right hooks to my jaw. I lifted my paw and, not being used to such fine tuning, my tap on his cheek bowled him over on his side. "Thanks, Dork," he said. "But I think we'll leave it at that for now. Trying to duplicate everything Joella did so well might be a slight to her memory."

If my attempts to impersonate Joey had been better, perhaps Xerxes might have kept going. But soon he said—the last thing he ever said to me—"Durf, I can't see going on like this any longer without her."

After that, the only sounds he made were those long, mournful meows, which became more frequent as they went down in volume. In an attempt to revive his spirits a little, That Man would pick him up and play him like an accordion. Xerxes seemed to still like it, but his purrs were nowhere near as loud as in the past. After a while, whenever That Man picked him up to play him, he just lay limp in his hands and stopped purring altogether.

No amount of my licking his face or nosing him was working either. I knew it was all over the time I lay down on my stomach so that Xerxes was between my paws, and he didn't reach up and bat my mouth softly with his blue, furry-between-toes paw.

Then one day, That Man put Xerxes in his travelling cage. "I'll give the vet your love, Durf, and tell her you're all right," he said on his way out. "She's going to be worried, because you haven't been in for a long while to get patched up." She worried? For an hour I lay around the house alone, worried sick because Xerxes hadn't even protested when he was placed in the cage.

An hour later, they came back in the house. After he'd put Xerxes down on his cushion, I heard That Man arranging a conference call with the rest of the family for that afternoon. Nice Girl and Nice Boy were still away, and Nice Woman had recently left for a few months to resume studies overseas.

The phone conversation began on a cheerful note and then turned sad. "Yes, it's heart-rending," said That Man into the receiver. "But the vet says it's our only humane option. She says he's in great pain, both mental and physical." He placed the receiver next to Xerxes's ear for a minute and his head moved a little in interest at what he was hearing from the other end. He made three weak meows, one for each beloved human.

When they all finished speaking to me, That Man said goodbye and hung up the phone. Then he crouched down and put his arm around my neck. "Durfy, you need to say goodbye to our beautiful Xerxes, too," he said. "The vet is going to have to do what is best for him."

I licked That Man's hand in agreement. I could not bear any longer watching what my poor Xerxes was going through. When I nuzzled his fluffy cheek gently and said a soft, "Wuff," meaning,

"I love you, Herpes, goodbye," he opened his lids a little and looked at me for a few seconds. I believe those golden eyes of his said to me, "Bye-bye, Dorky-Durfy, I love you, too." Yes, I know they did.

Chapter 21

The Parting of Ways

Seeing That Man going out the door again, with Xerxes lying silently in his cage, finished me altogether. It was sad enough having Nice Boy and Nice Girl and Nice Woman away from home, but they called often, and whenever they did they always talked to me. I knew they would be back home again to see me sooner or later. So, although their absence was a strain, I could live with it. And I had kept Joey's death from affecting me as badly as it had hit Xerxes, because I realized I had to be brave and show leadership to the others in our grief.

Now, though, with Xerxes checking out for good, on top of Joey being gone forever, it all just became too big a burden for me to carry. Every place in the house where either Joey or Xerxes used to eat, play, snooze, make sarcastic comments, perform naughty tricks, sit and lick their paws, or plan disasters with me, now seemed to be a dark cold cavern of emptiness. And there were too many of them.

I started to develop hip dysplasia. The vet said it was certainly age-related and probably genetic. That Man said that I should have chosen my mommy and daddy more carefully. Years ago, he used to say the same thing about the kink in my tail, and Nice Boy would have to respond that he was only joking and I shouldn't let it hurt my feelings. And Joey used to say, "There's enough blame to go around there, Dorky. We all fell down on the job when it came to picking our parents. But luckily we're bad-minded enough to overcome most of what we got."

When That Man added to my blame for my hips by saying that I should stop growing old, too, I knew he had to be joking again because, if any of us could stop growing old, a know-it-all like him would be doing it himself. Instead, he was well into his forties, and getting ancient and grumpy. Case in point: that time I tugged him along as I limped and crippled my way toward the new girl dog on the block to exchange sniffs with her, and he said to me, "I wish Mrs. Rock were here to tell you to act your age, Durf. You're getting too old for that."

What? Too old for romance? Me? Oh, I still loved That Man dearly and so forth, but for him to say something like that, I figured he must be going downhill fast. Until I remembered that I often heard him talking old romantic foolishness to Nice Woman on the phone. So we're seeing here a clear case of a man who aspired to be leader, yet who did not practise what he preached. Either that or he was frivolous enough to joke to me about something as serious as love. I worried about how he was going to cope when I was gone.

Maybe my parents and my age were in fact causing my sad condition, but there was more. I felt wretched because my buddies were no longer here for me to lead and protect and play games with. So, no matter what medicine or nutrition or exercise I received, I felt as if it was all pointless. Everything was futile.

Surgery was not a sensible option at my age, the vet said, and I was content with that. I just didn't mind anything, anymore.

Sometimes, if my hips weren't too painful, That Man would help me aboard the car and we'd drive up to Signal Hill and go for a walk there. I had no urge to run way down to the end of the Burma Road to see if my ancient pizza miracle had happened again—some other dog or fox could work that miracle now— and I had no desire to jump in and frolic about the lovely bog, or careen down over sheer cliffs and snigger to myself as That Man nearly croaked with anxiety. Those good old days were past. I was content now to amble along, slow enough to make sure he could keep up with me.

When I saw the eagles soaring above their nest in the valley, I felt no urge to run down and look at the eaglets in the nest. And it was not because of what That Man said to me, cheeky as usual: "I'm glad to see you learned your lesson about going too close to the eagles' nest." It was because I was happy just watching them soaring unhurriedly about on their wide wings. I longed to be flying everywhere on wings like them, until it came to me that they were probably looking down and wishing they could be walking along this trail with That Man, and sniffing excellent smells, like me. Just being up there on the hill, leading him along the trails, admiring the familiar sights, and taking in through my nose the beautiful old odours of seagulls and crows and eagles and foxes and rabbits and other dogs, and the occasional dead, decaying something—that made everything worthwhile.

When the kids and Nice Woman came home for the Christmas holidays, their presence made life good again, and sometimes I would forget the pain in my hips until I tried to romp around them. But most of the time I was glad I was alive to see them and feel their pats. And hear That Man's "jokes" to them: "Christmas is just not the same; Durf didn't climb the Christmas tree once."

Then, after they'd left to go back to wherever, the worst possible thing happened to me. I embarrassed myself by accidentally leaving a mess behind me on the kitchen floor. It was the first time in my life that this had happened in the house, after I'd been toilet trained as a puppy.

I couldn't have imagined myself doing something like that in my worst nightmares—me, the battler of bull moose, storm sewers, kidnappers, savage dogs, snowdrifts, swimming pools, yes—and valiant explorer of trails and streets and alleys and backlots and dumpsters and graveyards—a proud dog like me, the top dog in the place, doing such a thing right in my own house. I was mortified beyond measure. But I hadn't been able to help it. It just happened. Even That Man, as quick to judge me as he used to be, knew that. He patted me and said, "It's all right, old Durfy, it's okay." And he cleaned the mess up, making such a face of disgust on him, though, that I worried if he really had the right stuff to take over all the challenging responsibilities of top dog if anything ever happened to me.

I went out to the vet with him again for the second-last time. I knew something was seriously wrong when she just patted me and said, "Good boy," without saying a single comical thing to me, like, "Durf, have you been sick or something? It's been over a month since we had to sew you up." She examined me and X-rayed me and probed me and then said, "He's got inoperable cancer of the bowel. Together with the hip dysplasia, the pain is bad enough now, and it's only going to get worse and worse. Even with painkillers, his life will only be one continuous misery. I would advise a nice, long, peaceful sleep."

Sounded about right to me. But That Man said, "What? Another long sleep for Durf? No way. He's already spent most of his life asleep."

I looked at him and thought, *Don't tell me he's going back to his old contrary self again.* I'd hoped I'd trained him out of that. Heaven knew I'd put enough effort into it over the years.

The vet laughed and took my head between her two hands and said, "A good thing he *was* asleep now and then. Otherwise, he would have been here even more often."

That Man laughed, too, and gave me a man-hug with one arm. Everything was back to our normal fun. "I'll take him home for one last time," he said, "and call the family tonight so that they can have a little chat with him. I'll bring him back here tomorrow, if that's all right." He and the vet arranged the time, and I breathed a sigh of relief.

That night was wonderful. First, I spoke to Nice Woman and Nice Boy and Nice Girl on the phone. That Man held the receiver to my ear while each of them said lovely things to me, real poetry, like: "I love you, Durfy-doodles." It reminded me of when I was a child.

Then Granny and Mrs. Rock dropped in out of the blue. Ever since Nice Boy and Nice Girl had left the nest, Mrs. Rock had gone to work with Granny and Grampy because, in human years, they were nearly as old as me and needed some extra help about the house. Granny said, "Zippo is sorry you're feeling poorly, Durf, and he asked me to tell you that he forgives you for the way you bungled the Great Baked Ham Caper." That Zippo—what a card!

Mrs. Rock said, "I see you've finally started to act your age, Durf. But I liked it better when you looked like you were getting away with murder." It served no purpose now, but for old time's sake, I gave her the face. "Oh my glory," she said, clapping her hands, "he's still doing it."

After we'd had fun like that for a few minutes, and they left, That Man gave me a delicious ball of raw hamburger meat. It would make my night more comfortable, he said. If that was what the white pill in it was for, it didn't do much good, because I swallowed the meat and left the pill in my dish. Which made him say, "Amazing. I'd forgotten how good you were at wolfing down broken eggs and leaving the clean shells on the floor." And he added, "Besides which, of course, there's method to your madness, as usual. You get this extra prize." He wrapped the pill in another ball of hamburger and told me to swallow it all down whole this time. And I did it, so as not to undermine his self-esteem as a developing top dog. He didn't really have to hold my jaws shut until I'd swallowed the works.

Before I drifted off to sleep on the floor in his arms, he assured me that he was going to have me tell my life story, as we'd agreed, but he did have one question: Did I want to paper over my faults, and downplay my failings and shortcomings, or should they be described exactly like they were?

I hope I got it across to him with my eyes that it would not be necessary to tone down my shortcomings and faults, because, frankly, I didn't remember having any. He must have been thinking of Joey and Xerxes. And when it came to describing what those two lovable rogues had been up to, we had to tell everything precisely as it happened, because if we started holding back on their faults and deficiencies, they'd hardly be in the book at all. And that wouldn't be fair. As for my story, it should be told like it was: everything true, just like I'd tell it myself.

The next morning, when I woke up I was ready to go back

to the vet, and I hobbled and shuffled to the door and out to the car. That Man lifted me in. For the first time in my life—I was so surprised you could have knocked me over with a feather—he didn't make one remark about my weight.

When we got to the animal hospital, we were ushered right inside. That Man and the vet lifted me up on the padded table. She said she was going to give me a little sedative to make me relax, and within seconds I lay comfortably down on my side. The vet took off my leash and handed it to That Man. He said, "Don't worry Durf, this is not for another dog. No other dog would be able to take your place. We'll just keep the leash as a souvenir of the best dog in the world." I tried to wag my tail. I hope it worked. I think I felt it moving, kink and all. That Man's two hands were on my back and chest. "Give our love to Xerxes and Joey," he said. "Tell them we'll all miss you guys forever."

I will, I thought, gazing into his eyes and feeling myself drifting peacefully away. I hoped he was able to read in my eyes my last advice to him before he took over. *Whenever you have any questions or doubts about what to do as top dog in a difficult situation, Nice Man, you only need to ask yourself, "What would our Durfy do?"*

Author's Note

When our children were growing up, they had a dog and two cats who lived in our home for years as part of our family. The dog thought he was the boss of the two cats.

Much later, my wife and I entertained our grandchildren by telling them stories of the wild and comical antics, and poignant experiences, of those beloved pets. Our grandchildren's reaction—often amused, sometimes sad, and always fascinated—motivated me to write this book.

The dog and two cats who are the main characters in this book have the same names as our children's actual pets. And the stories here, though fictional as written, are based largely on events that actually occurred. All the human characters, however, are wholly fictional. This is emphasized by the fact that the novel is narrated by the dog and is told entirely from the point of view of himself and his two feline "partners in crime."

The book was written for dog and cat lovers of all ages who, as children or grown-ups, have laughed and sighed and cried over their pets.

Bill Rowe, St. John's
Newfoundland and Labrador, August 2015

Acknowledgements

As always, my sincere thanks to Garry, Margo, and Jerry Cranford, and to Laura Cameron, Peter Hanes, Bob Woodworth, Randy Drover, Grant Loveys, and Gerard Murphy, all of Flanker Press, for the generous roles they played in the editing, publishing, marketing, and distribution of the book. And once more, my wholehearted thanks to graphic designer Graham Blair for creating the delightful covers.

Also my heartfelt appreciation to my wife, Penny, and our son and daughter, Dorian and Toby, for recalling many of the antics of Durf, Xerxes, and Joey that have been fictionalized here, and to acclaimed writer Donna Morrissey for her encouragement as I wrote about them.

THE TRUE CONFESSIONS OF
A BADLY
MISUNDERSTOOD
DOG

The original Durf, caught strewing laundry about the house

The original Joey studying Xerxes's fur close up

The original Durf "cooling off" in the backyard

The original Durf putting on the face
that "gets him off with murder every time"

The original Durf unaware of Joey behind him, plotting

The original Durf at the pool where his namesake "rescued" That Man

The original Durf emerging from hiding under a bed

The original Durf looking embarrassed by the attention of the
original Xerxes

Not as good as a yummy cookbook,
but a piece of wood will do in a pinch.

The author carrying the original Durf away from some calamity

Born in Newfoundland, Bill Rowe graduated in English from Memorial University and attended Oxford University as a Rhodes Scholar, obtaining an Honours M.A. in law.

Elected five times to the House of Assembly, Rowe served as a minister in the Government of Newfoundland and Labrador and as leader of the Official Opposition. He practised law in St. John's for many years and has been a long-time public affairs commentator, appearing regularly on national and local television, as well as hosting a daily radio call-in show on VOCM and writing weekly newspaper columns.

Rowe has written nine books: *Clapp's Rock*, a bestselling novel published by McClelland & Stewart and serialized on CBC national radio; *The Temptation of Victor Galanti*, a second novel published by McClelland & Stewart; a volume of essays on politics and public affairs published by Jesperson Press of St. John's; the critically acclaimed political memoir *Danny Williams: The War With Ottawa*, which appeared on the *Globe and Mail*'s bestsellers list in 2010; *Danny Williams, Please Come Back*, a collection of newspaper articles covering social, political, and economic issues; *Rosie O'Dell*, a critically acclaimed crime novel published by Pennywell Books, a literary imprint of Flanker Press; *The Premiers Joey and Frank*, which was a *Globe and Mail* bestseller in 2013, and which the *Hill Times* selected as one of the Best 100 Books in Politics, Public Policy, and History in 2013; *The Monster of Twenty Mile Pond*, the much-loved novel of a legendary monster who engulfed the lives of two teenaged girls; and now *The True Confessions of a Badly Misunderstood Dog*, a fictionalized account of the frantic years when a Labrador retriever and two cats lived with the author's family.

Rowe is a member of the Writers' Union of Canada and has served on the executive of the Writers' Alliance of Newfoundland and Labrador. He is married to Penelope Ayre Rowe CM of St. John's. They have a son, Dorian, a daughter, Toby, and three grandchildren, Rowan, Elizabeth, and Phoebe.

Visit Flanker Press at:

www.flankerpress.com

https://www.facebook.com/flankerpress

https://twitter.com/FlankerPress

http://www.youtube.com/user/FlankerPress